THE ENEMY RETURNS

Instinctively, TC Creighton knew something was terribly wrong. "What's happened?"

"Perhaps I should have let you kill Benhaddou last year." Shona's voice was soft. "Had I not interfered, those men would be alive. And others might not be killed by my brother."

TC recalled trapping and crippling Benhaddou in the desert after the Morocc slaughtered his wife. He wanted to kill the man, but Shona pleaded, not for Benhaddou's life: for Creighton's salvation.

TC shook his head. "What have you learned about his escape? Has he been found?"

"He has many disguises. We must be cautious."

TC looked suddenly at the nomad prophet. "Why do you say that?"

"The camp was searched. They found nothing. Except one thing."

"Tell me, goddammit!" TC demanded.

"Silver's grave. Her grave was defiled. He took her body."

★ ★ ★ ★ ★ ★ ★ ★ ★ ★ ★ ★ ★

Also by Bill Dolan

AFRIKORPS
IRON HORSE

Published by
HarperPaperbacks

BILL DOLAN

AFRIKORPS

WHITE RHINO

HarperPaperbacks
A Division of HarperCollins*Publishers*

HarperPaperbacks   *A Division of* HarperCollins*Publishers*
10 East 53rd Street, New York, N.Y. 10022

Copyright © 1992 by HarperCollins*Publishers*
All rights reserved. No part of this book may be used or reproduced in any manner whatsoever without written permission of the publisher, except in the case of brief quotations embodied in critical articles and reviews. For information address HarperCollins*Publishers*,
10 East 53rd Street, New York, N.Y. 10022.

Cover illustration by Danilo Ducak

First printing: March 1992

Printed in the United States of America

HarperPaperbacks and colophon are trademarks of HarperCollins*Publishers*

❖ 10 9 8 7 6 5 4 3 2 1

For Grover and Rose Gardner,
Huntsville, Alabama

Foreword

★★★★★★★★

2176 A.D.

North Africa, in the area once called Morocco, had officially been deemed Quadrant One by the International Commission now mandated to oversee the pacification of the continent. The Commission was composed of representatives from the European continent and the United States; all were members of the multinational military task force designated *AfriKorps.*

The MNF was now unified under the command of the General Staff, which was headed by the Supreme Commander, U.S. Army Colonel Thomas Clayton. The General Staff was composed of officers from each nation; the Supreme Commander reported directly to the Commission.

The composition of the AfriKorps had changed nearly as fast as the topography; nearly as fast as the southern advance. By September, 2176, what was once the most lush part of Africa—the west-central region devastated by the Cataclysm of the twenty-first century—was beginning to revitalize.

Grass was growing, and with the gradual rise of rivers, savannah grasslands were beginning to grow. Trees brought from the biomes in the United States were being planted by the hundreds of thousands. Water was becoming more plentiful as the nearly completed desalinization plant on the west coast of Quadrant One pumped fresh water through pipelines to where a large riverbed had dried out during the Cataclysm.

The nightmare wasn't over, but the earth was being forced to awaken from its deep sleep that had nearly erased human beings from its surface.

A railroad track cut through the desert to the eastern border of the Quadrant; the border of what was once Egypt. The track was now being extended south, toward the hostile-controlled region that was next on Clayton's pacification list: Quadrant Two, the middle of the African continent.

The railroad train, called "Iron Horse" by all who saw the technologically advanced rapid deployment weapons platform, was now composed of three trains. Designated Marge, Francine, and Zada, each train operated in its own region.

Marge was deployed to the east of Quadrant One.

Francine was deployed from south of AfriKorps Base Camp One to the border of Quadrant One and Quadrant Two.

Zada was pushing through the south into the heart of Quadrant Two behind the track-laying gang, still called by its historical designation of "steel gang" though the track was now laid by technological automation and not by sweat and muscle.

In advance of Zada were recon elements probing the hostile territory. They conducted mapping and reconnaissance missions, as well as friendly pacification with the indigenous survivors who had banded together and formed various tribes.

The pacification teams, or PT's, were an important phase of AfriKorps duty. Clayton had ordered that an

"Iron Necklace" be gradually extended to the south, providing food, medical care, and protection to the indigenous tribes.

His philosophy was simple: why kill them if they would become allies. Tribes were pacified, trained in weaponry, thus providing a stationary military presence in a particular sector of the Quadrant.

This allowed the special operations squadrons of AfriKorps to push farther and faster to the south, rolling up the hostiles called Marauders from the southern region.

Intelligence gathering determined that during the Cataclysm several biospheres in the former Republic of South Africa had been penetrated by hostiles from the outside. The hostiles forced the biosphere inhabitants to share their knowledge and technology; then they were destroyed when no longer useful.

But the greatest weapon of all was still not plentiful: food. The Marauders, with their tanks and weapons, began a push north to invade the more lush farmland of Europe, destroying and enslaving every living thing in their path.

From the United States was dispatched the DESFOR, the Desert Forces of the Western biospheres under Clayton's command. His orders: Stop the slaughter. Pacify Africa.

This is the continuing story of that operation code-named *AfriKorps*!

Prologue

September 22, 2176.

The old man had first been taken to the cave as a child. Eventually abandoned after the death of the man who had brought him there, he often tried to understand how he had survived. The answer never came. It was as though the spirit he had heard beseeched as a youngster had intervened.

God!

The survivors spoke of God, and it was said that He was great. But the old man, whose name was Ibo, had long forgotten the stories told of this spirit called God; stories that died from around the evening firelight as the people gradually died.

He had spent most of his life alone, except for the time when the young woman had come into his life, and that had been only for a short time.

Like him, her hair was short, coarse; and their skin was black. Black as the sky that was once visible at night but that had gradually become lost as a curtain of foul poison had risen from the earth, turning the sky a deep yellow.

There the line had been drawn: a divider between the Heaven of the distant sky and the Hell on earth that was called the Cataclysm.

That was many years ago when his hands were young and strong, not feeble twists of bone and skin that

1

looked like dried vine; when his muscles rippled, and before his hair turned white.

He had kept track of the seasons with a notch on the wall of the cave. They now added up to over one hundred. He had been there at the beginning of the Cataclysm, when the earth suddenly refused to provide a safe environment for its caretakers: man.

And there was danger. As the earth died, so did the people who inhabited the region in the west-central part of Africa that was called Nigeria. Like others, he had gone to the mountains to the east and sought refuge from the wandering bands of scavengers who roamed the land in search of food; in search of survival.

How he had survived he did not know. He had watched the grass die, then the trees. Water had become scarce, except for an underground stream that flowed through the cave. The water's sweetness had gradually turned brackish and tasted like the air.

But he had learned to drink the foul water; he had learned how to breathe the foul air. He had learned how to live with the worst of the conditions created by the Cataclysm: loneliness.

But again, he told himself, he had survived. He had outlasted the horror. Standing at the mouth of his cave, he saw something he remembered from childhood; what had been missing for over a century: grass.

The land was turning a velvety green; a green that stretched from the plain in the west to the hills where he saw trees growing. Creatures were flying and he remembered that they were called birds.

He thought again while trying to answer the mystery by recalling the tales of how the earth began. He thought of the spirit called God and wondered if the Great One's thirst for vengeance had been quenched.

Have we paid enough?

The sun was now on the horizon and the cool night air stung his skin. He retreated into the cave and sat on the stone where he had spent most of his life waiting, pondering, wondering what would happen next; keeping alive the wisdom of the past while hoping it might be useful again in the future.

On the wall, drawn carefully by the man who had brought him to the cave as a child, was the image of an animal he had seen only once. The animal's skin, he had been told by the man, was as tough as rock. A large horn sat on its snout, one that brought great power if removed and ground to powder.

The man, whom Ibo figured was his father, had said that the animal was called the Rhino, named for the horn sought for its magical power.

Looking at the image, he studied the outline, the powerful shoulders, short muscular legs, long trunk, and massive frame. But what made it intriguing, most interesting, was its color was not white. Like the black rhino, it had the same color. However, the white rhino's trunk was longer, and from the side appeared wider. The African word for 'wide' sounded like the English word 'white.' Therefore, the rhino became known as the 'white rhino.'

It had been, the man had said, the last one on the earth. But he also said that one day God might return to earth, and bring the White Rhino back to Africa with him. Should that day come, the man had said, Ibo must be ready to protect and help preserve the creature's future. So they lived in the cave and the man taught Ibo about the White Rhino, and to be prepared should the animal return. The days turned into years; the years into decades. One day the man left the cave and never returned. Ibo remained, waiting. Each day he studied the drawing and recited the instructions he had committed to memory. He drank the brackish water, ate what food he could find, mostly insects and reptiles, and avoided the other survivors who roamed the hills searching for food and water.

They were vicious, these survivors. They had killed the young woman who once shared his cave and had

probably killed his father. He had fought for his life on
many occasions, using the club the man had left in the
cave. It had a long smooth shaft made of metal and a
wooden head that could split a human skull.

But that was when he was young; now he was old and
ran whenever he saw humans. Especially the ones in the
next valley who looked like the young woman, except
they were larger and ferocious. They were not gentle
like his woman. Which was why on this night, he slipped
farther into the rear of the cave.

In the next valley the firelight rose and licked the
black night; red embers would drift upward, cool, then
explode, leaving a momentary signature, then drift back
to ground as ash.

Thirty women lay around the fires, their black skin
ashen from the residue collecting on the sweaty sheen
coating their bodies. Beneath the women lay the men
who had come from the south; strong, white-skinned,
with blue eyes and hair the color of the sun. But they
were evil, thought Neshu, the woman who was the leader of the tribe. She didn't trust the men that had found
their valley only two days before.

The white men had been passing through for nearly a
year, journeying north with their loud, groaning
machines that looked like turtles as they moved across
the earth. Tanks, the one had said. They were from the
tribe called Marauders. It was a name she had heard as
the whites crept from the south.

Neshu had kept her tribe out of sight. There were
only thirty, all women and a few children, all female offspring from the annual rite of the previous season.

Now there was new blood to mix with theirs. The
blood of the whites, who seemed anxious to share their
life-creating fluids with the tall, slender women of her
tribe. And what man could resist? The women were
known for their beauty, strength, courage—and for their
fiery passion on the night of the annual ritual. The
autumn day when sun and moon shared the sky in equal

portions. Which was why they were called the Equinox
Women.

"The day began with you in my arms," she whispered
to the man, whose body was as firm as hers, though
shorter. At six-foot four, Neshu was not the tallest of the
Equinox Women, but she was certainly the strongest.

"And it shall end with you in my arms," she continued.

The man, whose name she had forgotten, lay pinned
by her powerful hands. With each orgasm, he noticed
she seemed to grow stronger. By afternoon he was
sapped, but she continued to ride him, driving her
knees into his rib cage.

He was certain he wouldn't walk for a week. When he
tried to speak, her fingertip touched his mouth, quiet-
ing him. She leaned back, rubbed the muscles of his
thighs and threw back her head.

Her long hair, in ropelike braids, whipped through
the air. A moment later, there were other similar sounds.
Trying to rise, the man saw around the fires the women
riding his men, their heads moving in a circular motion,
whipping the air with their braids.

It was spectacular, he thought. The sound reminded
him of the antennae on his tank, whipping at night as
they sat in bivouac in a windstorm. Around and around
their heads twirled, their braids flying out in circles.

The sound of Neshu moaning was joined by the
moans of the other women. A crescendo rose into the
night until there was a steady drone of the moaning that
seemed to cause the earth to move.

The man suddenly felt himself become frightened.
He tried to rise but her size and strength overpowered
him. Her thighs tightened around his manhood, caus-
ing him pain. When she straightened over him he tried
to scream from the pain. But the words didn't come out.

He felt a tightness around his throat, and looking up,
saw in the moonlight her figure looming over him, her
head close to his, her braids gripped tightly in her fist.
The braids tightened around his throat, and he could

no longer feel the air filling his lungs. His fingers reached for the pistol, but his reach was too short.

The moan changed to a deep, guttural chuckle; the sound came from around the fire.

He was dying!

* * *

Ibo sat far back within the cave, listening to the moans wafting from the other valley which were finally replaced by the chuckling of the Equinox Women. He had heard the sound each season since the young woman had disappeared.

He was not frightened. He laid the metal shaft with the wooden head on the ground beside him and curled close against the wall.

Tonight he could sleep without fear. He would not have this night of safety again; not until the next season when again, on the day the sun and moon shared the sky equally, the Equinox Women would be satisfied by the lust—and lives—of their lovers.

He drifted off to sleep, dreaming of the day God would return the White Rhino to his valley.

★★★★★★★★★★★★★

PART ONE
ENEMIES

★★★★★★★

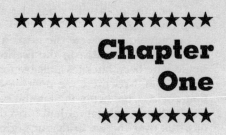

★★★★★★★★★★★★★

Chapter
One

★★★★★★★

**Biosphere One. Appalachian Mountains.
September 25, 2176.**

Woolford Dawson walked with a steady gait that seemed
to remove all hint of the limp he suffered as a younger
man; a younger man leading an expedition from North
America to Europe. That had been the 2155 Dawson
Expeditionary Force, an accomplishment he considered
more important than his current role as President of the
United States.

The presidency was political. The DEF was historical.
He might not be remembered as president. He would be
remembered as the first American to make contact with
the Europeans following the Cataclysm.

For more than a year he had agonized over the decision to send American troops into Africa at the request
of the European governments which were part of the
MNF. He had seen too much destruction on his continent to consider the idea of more Americans dying in
faraway lands. In the end he had agreed. Not because
there was that much for America to gain. Rather,
because it was the right thing to do.

If civilization was to recover from the destruction of
the Cataclysm, it would take the effort of all governments able and willing to lend assistance both technologically and militarily. Which was why he was interested
in meeting with the delegation from the Soviet Union.

Not because he would offer them military aid; that wasn't necessary.

Communications were the weakest link in the present-day world community. In the twenty-first century there would have been satellites available for instant global communication. Now there was only line-of-sight communication. Archaic, but better than nothing.

The Soviet delegation had arrived following an arduous trek over the ice bridge at Bering, where they were met by forces of MounFor near the old port of Anchorage. Anchorage lay beneath hundreds of feet of water, but the ice pack was firm and MounFor led the Soviets to Biosphere One without incident.

The hostiles in America had been eradicated; either killed or induced to change their ways through the Pioneer Program. The concept of the Pioneer Program was to resettle rehabilitated hostiles and return them to certain areas where they would become modern-day counterparts of the nineteenth century western.

From B-1, Dawson rode in the back seat of a Landrover to the experimental station ten miles from the biosphere. This was to be a very important morning. As he rode through the security gate he could see that the Soviets were waiting with anticipation, especially their leader.

At forty-one, Serge Valitnikov was a robust man who had risen to prominence, becoming the advisor to the Soviet President at the Moscow Biosphere, the seat of Soviet government. He was trim, with thick, dark hair and bushy eyebrows. There was something sinister about the man at first glance, but that impression soon dissolved as his character was gradually revealed.

"Good morning, Mr. President." Valitnikov extended his hand to the president as he marched forward from a group of scientists who had been working since 5:00 A.M.

A large octagonal-shaped sphere rose twenty feet into the morning sky; it seemed to bristle as the sun danced off the surface, which looked like the skin of a snake.

"What do you think, Serge?" the president asked as he pointed at what was called GroundStar.

"It's magnificent, Mr. President." He spoke without pausing, and Dawson knew the man was convinced. "I think my government will be more than willing to join the GroundStar project."

Dawson swelled with satisfaction. "Good. Then we'll be able to establish a worldwide communication belt."

"'The Dawson Belt,' was what one of your scientists called the project." The Soviet smiled pleasantly as Dawson became flushed.

"I could think of a better name," the president grumbled.

"Nonsense. You're too modest. It's magnificent." He pointed from east to west, drawing a circle through the air as he spoke. "Each GroundStar station will have a range of 250 miles in all directions. With a belt of these stations beginning here, crossing America, then extending into Russia, through Europe and into Africa, we will link three-fourths of the world land mass with immediate communications. Not since the Cataclysm has earth had such capability."

Dawson was pleased. Taking the lead, he walked to the GroundStar station where he was met by several scientists, one of whom was an old friend.

Dr. Paul Shoemaker and Woolford Dawson had grown up in Biosphere One, which the children had referred to as Uranus, the Father of Titans. Shoemaker had accompanied the Dawson expedition into Europe to the tip of Spain, and it was on that journey that Shoemaker first conceived the notion of the GroundStar project.

GroundStar was designed to be placed in areas of high elevation, capable of transmitting from station to station on a low-frequency wavelength, thus reestablishing worldwide communications. All that was required was government cooperation and training of the technicians who would man the stations. The Soviet Union was to be the linchpin in the project, the critical centerpiece of GroundStar.

Inside the sphere, banks of radio transmitters and receivers lined the circular wall. There was a steady hum from the ceiling, which all recognized as coming from the charging of the solar batteries; batteries built into the panels where solar energy was stored from the outer skin that fed on the sun's heat.

"We're ready when you are, Mr. President." Shoemaker handed Dawson a microphone.

Stations had been erected in a line from Biosphere One to the new station inside Siberia on the Soviet coast near the Bering Sea.

"This is President Woolford Dawson, president of the United States. With whom am I speaking?"

The signal skipped from station to station, across the Continental Divide, up the Pacific West Coast to a station near Nome, and relayed across the Bering Strait to the Soviet station sent to that part of the world three months ago.

"*Do'braye oo'tra!* Good morning, Mr. President." The voice replied in soft Russian. It was a woman's voice.

"Good morning." Dawson's suddenly sounded excited. It was the first time in over a century that two people had communicated from one hemisphere to the next.

An hour later, pleased with the success, Dawson walked with Shoemaker. The president knew that GroundStar was important for diplomatic purposes, but there were other applications where it could prove vital to American interests and most importantly—to American lives.

"Paul, I want you to begin preparation for installing GroundStar where it's needed most."

Shoemaker shrugged. "The Soviets are being cooperative. We can have the trans-Siberian link into Europe within six months."

Dawson shook his head. "No. That's not where it's needed the most. You can have that project run by your people and the Soviets. Right now it's needed in a more vital area. At the other end."

Shoemaker stopped in his tracks. "Africa?"

Dawson kept walking toward a large building as he said, "Africa. Our troops can put the system to work immediately in that theater of operation."

Shoemaker said nothing. He knew an order when he heard it.

Dawson pointed to the building, which was the size of an old football field and heavily guarded by a security fence and armed guards.

"What's the situation with this project?"

Shoemaker grinned. "See for yourself."

The two men entered the building and went to an open area where twenty technicians stood surrounding an object draped in white cloth.

"Remove the cover," Dawson ordered.

In the next second his heart nearly stopped.

"My God . . . it's magnificent." He walked around the sleek machine, which he could see was designed to carry only one passenger.

The cockpit of Thunder One, the first aircraft built in over a century, sat squat against the floor, its solar skin gleaming beneath the artificial lights from the ceiling.

"What's the flying time?" the president asked.

"Two hours, at the present. With full combat load, I might add. Clean and empty, there's another hour flying time."

The aircraft looked like a wing. The skin was designed to absorb solar energy that fed the batteries which operated the power plants, two propeller-driven engines mounted aft of each wing. Beneath the wing hung a black gun pod; the muzzle of a 30mm cannon protruded from it.

"When can you have one of these ready for the field?" asked the president.

"The aircraft can be disassembled and crated for shipping within twenty-four hours." Shoemaker motioned to one of the scientists.

Flight Officer Captain Alissa Breen walked forward. She carried a strange-looking helmet. Dawson knew the helmet encompassed the sighting mechanism that operated Thunder One's weapons systems.

Shoemaker introduced her to the president. "This is the pilot of the Thunder Project. She is the only person I'd trust to field-test the aircraft."

Dawson looked at Breen, a beautiful blonde with green eyes, and knew the answer even before he posed the question.

"Have you ever been to Africa?"

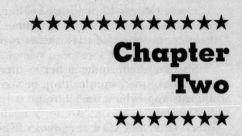

★★★★★★★★★★★★★

Chapter Two

★★★★★★★

Base Camp One. AfriKorps Headquarters.
October 30, 2176.
0900.

His name was Benhaddou, and if there was such a thing as pure evil, it was the man who sat in the maximum security cell in the prison at Base Camp One. The brother of Shona, and former leader of the Moroccs, Benhaddou had been captured after cutting a murderous swath through the AfriKorps.

The military tribunal that sat in judgement at his trial had considered the death penalty, but after reflection, thought the greatest punishment a man could suffer would be total incarceration in a small cell for the rest of his natural life.

After nearly a year in the cell, Benhaddou agreed completely. Death would have been a blessing compared to what he was forced to endure.

Benhaddou was tall, black skinned, with dark eyes that flamed at the three television security cameras on the wall of his cell. He seemed to sense another person watching him from the master console at the end of the hallway where his cell, and six others all empty, composed the maximum security wing of the stockade.

Captain Abraham "TC" Creighton also had dark eyes, and they were never more hate-filled than now as he leaned toward the television screen, watching the prisoner.

15

The security guard, a young soldier Creighton had grown up with in the Vegas Biosphere in the Western Quadrant, watched TC. He understood the soldier's hate.

"He's like a bug under a microscope, TC. He can't turn around, stand up, sit down, or take a leak without someone watching him." The guard shrugged. "I'd rather be dead."

"You better not take your eyes off him, Tyler. That man could slip through a crack in the wall." His thoughts raced back to Silver, his bride of only weeks, whom Benhaddou had murdered and raped.

Tyler's voice grew soft. He knew what the tank commander was thinking. "We won't. He'll live in that concrete and steel cage until he dies of old age. That's a promise."

Creighton took one more look at the prisoner. He studied his physique, which was strong and powerful looking.

"He appears to be in good shape."

Tyler stood and poured a glass of water. "He exercises nearly two-thirds of the day. The rest of the day he spends reading. He's learning to write and he picked up our language faster than anything I've seen. Not just spoken. But written language. It's amazing."

TC thought of the prisoner's brother, TC's friend Shona. "He comes from exceptional stock. Too bad he wasn't more like his brother."

Creighton checked his watch and then turned to leave. "Better go, Tyler. Keep an eye on the bastard. I'll see you when I get back."

"Going out on patrol?"

TC nodded. "Yeah. Quadrant Two. Hamp's come up with another of his crazy notions."

Tyler laughed. He knew Hamp Floris was the agronomy specialist assigned to AfriKorps. He had built a farm on Base Camp One that was called Hamp's Farm, producing vegetables and other fruits. He had also begun a tree-planting project throughout the Pacific desert region of Quadrant One. Life was being returned to earth by the descendants of those who had once destroyed it. TC turned and passed through a glass door designed to stop an explosive charge. He looked back one more time, through the glass door at the television screen. The prisoner was staring at the video camera in his cell.

A cold chill swept along TC's spine as he stared at the face of Benhaddou. TC thought he saw the man smiling at him.

★★★★★★★★★★★★★
Chapter
Three
★★★★★★★

Colonel Thomas Clayton was a stout man with gray hair, the only suggestion that he was nearly fifty years old. Stepping from the shower in his private apartment connected to his office at the newly constructed AfriKorps General Command Headquarters, he towelled himself dry and opened a fresh packet of the standard-issue desert camouflage fatigues. These were made of biodegradable material that would ultimately dissolve after a certain period.

After dressing, he went into his office and began signing reports that would be dispatched to the Commission. The reports concerned the desalinization plant, and contained a recommendation memorandum requesting a second and third plant be built in the United States and shipped to Africa for assembly.

Water was the most important ingredient on the continent, along with the spare parts for the armored units carrying the fight to the Marauders.

Other reports included a request from Hamp Floris. He chuckled at the notion, but realized Hamp's request was as much of a part of the AfriKorps mission as destroying the Marauders. So he signed the request along with the others and sealed the paperwork in a pouch that would be given a priority dispatch to the president of the United States at Biosphere One.

He looked up as his door opened. TC Creighton,

along with the gunner on his tank, Sergeant Steve
Puhaly, walked in without knocking.

"Be seated, gentlemen." Clayton nodded at two
chairs.

The air-conditioning felt good against Puhaly's skin.
He was a short, muscular man with a mustache set in a
weathered, sun-bronzed face. He had even begun wearing his slightly thinning hair in a ponytail, tied in the
back with a length of rope that could quickly be turned
into a garrote. Puhaly always cut the sleeves out of his
fatigue shirts, and after years of ridicule from Clayton
and other officers, was no longer bothered for the dress
code infraction. He was his own man; own soldier.
Unconventional. Bawdy. But the man to have at your
side when the fight was the most intense.

Reaching to a projector, Clayton instantly flashed a
hologram onto the cool air of the room. What they saw
was a map of Africa, with the continent divided into
Quadrants; the Quadrants were divided into sectors.
The green sectors indicated pacified areas; yellow indicated nearly complete pacified areas. The red indicated
hostile areas. All of Quadrant One was green. The
northern sector of Quadrant Two was yellow. Below
that, the rest of the African continent was red.

Clayton put a pointer onto the map and followed a
line that stretched from Base Camp One to the yellow
border of Quadrant Two. "Captain Creighton, you and
your Lion squadron will deploy this afternoon to this
area. You'll relieve Captain Armbrust's Panther
squadron and continue with his mission."

Creighton understood. Commanded by newly promoted Captain Mike Armbrust, the Panther squadron
had been in the Quadrant providing support and security for the extending railroad, indicated by the black line
on the map.

Clayton paused. "You'll also be accompanied by
Hamp Floris and a team of zoologists."

There was a silence that made Clayton appear

uncomfortable. TC and Puhaly simply stared at the man as though he had made a mistake.

"Zoologists!" TC finally blurted.

"Correct. Zoologists."

"Why are zoologists going along?" Puhaly asked. He had his arms crossed; his right and left biceps flexed alternately, a sign all recognized as a warning when he was irritated.

"Hamp has received approval on a project he submitted to the Commission a few months back. The first of several phases."

"What project?" asked Creighton.

"The project is to re-introduce certain species back into the wilds of Africa. Species that once inhabited the continent. The Science and Technology Institute at Biosphere One agree. It's their feeling the environs will increase proliferation if the natural chain is restored to a pre-Cataclysm state."

"Fine. But don't you think it's a little risky sending a research team south with an advancing element? Why not wait until the region is pacified?" asked Creighton.

"Mating," Clayton said flatly.

"Mating! What has mating got to do with it?" TC shook his head in dismay.

Clayton released a long sigh. "The animals targeted for the project mate during a certain time of the year. Then, of course, there's gestation and birth. The scientists feel it's better to have the first newborn generation conceived and born in the environment they'll be returning to. This will be experimentation, of course, similar to other projects in the United States, where animals are being reintroduced in North America."

"Jesus," said Puhaly. "I'd like to meet some of the pinheads who come up with these ideas. Our job is tough enough with fighting the Marauders and a continent filled with hostile elements. Now we have to baby-sit zoologists."

Clayton had a wicked grin on his face. "That's not all."

TC groaned. He could see the situation wasn't going to get better. "What else?"

"Captain Armbrust's squadron will be responsible for the animals . . . once they arrive at end of track. The farthest point south. Which means you'll assume his duty. The Panther squadron needs a break. Which leaves your Lion squadron. You'll have a dual mission."

"Which is?" TC asked acidly.

Clayton raised the pointer to the hologram. "Hamp intends to establish a closely guarded game reserve. Armbrust's reports indicate this area is the ideal location for the reserve in this part of the continent."

The pointer was touching near where there were two valleys in what was once Nigeria. "Your mission will be be twofold: first, assist Hamp and the zoologists with establishing secure boundaries in the reserve; secondly, you'll push south, establishing a buffer zone around the reserve. That includes pacifying hostiles and securing the area from any hostile threat. Armbrust's squadron will be in the rear, but in a state of readiness in the event you need a rapid deployment element. You'll mount your squadron here, aboard Francine, then proceed to where Zada will be waiting. You'll be there by midnight."

Clayton sat at his desk. "That's your mission."

"I'll need Reno's troop of IFV's with my squadron of MBT's. And I want Shona," said TC.

Creighton looked at his watch. "I figured as much. Reno and his troop left this morning to contact Shona. They've been instructed to meet you at a substation along the track."

"What about Hamp?" asked Puhaly. "And these zoologists?"

"You'll meet them at the debarkation station here at Base Camp One. Francine is scheduled to return within the hour. I suggest you begin loading as soon as the train arrives."

★★★★★★★★★★★★★

Chapter
Four

★★★★★★★

1300.

Hamp Floris had learned as a youngster that he had a green thumb and a love for animals. Perhaps these were hereditary traits. Throughout the Cataclysm, a Floris could be found in the agriculture biome, standing knee deep in one of the experimental fields, or in the zoology biome, bottle-feeding a new generation of animals. The most painful experience concerned the animals, since herds could not be raised in the biosphere. Only offspring were maintained, then painlessly put to death once they had mated. This method was necessary, though certainly not acceptable. But it kept the blood-lines of animals assigned to the Vegas Biosphere constant, producing a more viable offspring than artificial test tube re-creation.

Hamp, now forty-four, pushed his pince-nez glasses higher onto the bridge of his nose as he leaned over a microscope, studying the cellular structure of a blood sample. Beside him, two other scientists watched as the chief of AfriKorps Experimental Projects scrutinized the sample.

"No sign of disease," he said in a tone that sounded pleased. He wasn't necessarily surprised; most diseases had been eradicated in the biospheres, leaving only the threat of bacteria growing on the outside. Still, he knew he couldn't be too careful.

Placing another sample marked GNU under the microscope, he carefully studied the blood sample of the great animal that once roamed the continent. "A perfect pair. They are all in good condition."

Dr. Frank Sawyer, a zoologist from the St. Louis Biosphere, and Dr. Jean Peterson, from the Detroit Biosphere, watched with growing anticipation. The gnu, or wildebeest, sample was drawn only an hour before, the last to be tested from the forty species they had shipped from the United States.

The trio of scientists went to the rear of the building which housed the project. The smell of the animals was refreshing to Hamp; a smell he had missed since leaving Vegas.

Eighty cartons of various sizes stood in neat rows. The sounds of the animals, some banging against the cages, filled the air. A small group of soldiers stood watch; some were feeding the animals, others were bringing water. The atmosphere was one of awe—and excitement.

Walking along the rows, he stopped between the two largest cages. The structure was heavier than the others, and for good reason. Inside the cage stood a broad-shouldered animal that Hamp had only seen pictures of.

"These two are my favorites," Jean Peterson said proudly. A tall woman with a determined face, she knelt beside the cage labelled *Adam*. The opposite cage holding Adam's mate was labelled Eve.

Hamp knelt at the cage and reached through the bars. His hand patted the protruding snout of Adam. "He's beautiful," Hamp whispered.

The white rhino stared at the agronomist through eyes that seemed to be mystified.

★★★★★★★★★★★★★

Chapter Five

★★★★★★★

Quadrant One. Atlas Mountains. 1330.

The man called Shona sat at the entrance to a cave that he had lived in for over a decade. Since the arrival of the soldiers from America he had found the AfriKorps soldiers a friendly lot, with comforts that he found pleasing, such as the food, the water, and the air-cooled rooms where they slept on soft beds. He had been given his own quarters at Base Camp One, but from time to time returned to his cave to reacquaint himself with the world he had survived.

A deadly world.

The former chief only had to follow the incline leading down from the cave to find the evidence of how difficult it had been to survive. Skeletons lay strewn among the rocks; the bones of his former assassins lay bleached beneath the harsh sun.

Assassins sent by Benhaddou before his brother was captured and imprisoned by the AfriKorps.

When he heard the low-pitched whine in the distance, his first thought was that there might be Marauders in the area. Then he relaxed as a column of vehicles became visible on the narrow path winding through the ravine at the base of the incline.

An AfriKorps troops IFV's, infantry fighting vehicles, an AfriKorp troop, rolled to a halt. The vehicles were armed with devastating weapons; but nothing

compared to the greater MBT's main battle tanks, of the
AfriKorp.

The turret opened on the lead IFV and Shona sensed
he knew the man climbing down to the ground. Shona
grinned and stood, carrying a long spear as he started
down the incline.

Lieutenant Reno Falken was tall, rangy, with broad
shoulders, narrow hips, and flashing blue eyes concealed behind the solar visor that extended from his
fighting helmet. Reno stood waiting, certain that his
friend would know of their presence. Momentarily,
Shona appeared from behind a tall boulder. They
clasped each other's forearms in greeting.

Falken explained his reason for finding the nomad.
"Colonel Clayton respectfully requests your assistance in
a mission to the south."

"To what part of the south?"

Falken took out a map and spread it on the ground.
The map depicted the outline of the west coast of the
continent, including the coastal regions now redefined
since the rising waters of the Cataclysm had moved
inland, erasing a major chunk of the continent. His finger travelled along the black line indicating the railroad.
He stopped at the two valleys.

"Reports indicate this is the region the new project is
to be conducted. We'll establish an outpost, clear the
area of hostile activity, and extend the Iron Necklace."

"What about Marauders?" There was concern in his
voice, but he couldn't stop staring at the two valleys.

"Reconnaissance reports indicate the Marauders have
switched strategy. They aren't pushing north. Clayton
believes they're planning to establish a defensive posture on a line running east and west in this area in the
southern part of Quadrant Two. That's well south of the
outpost. We need you to be our interpreter."

Shona nodded that he understood. "To continue the
Iron Necklace to the south."

Iron Necklace was Clayton's plan to approach the

tribes of nomads in the area, pacify them, then use them
as defensive forces against the Marauders. This eliminat-
ed the need for vast numbers of MNF troops, and kept
the AfriKorps on the move, pushing the Marauders
deeper into the continent.

"Have you been in that area?" asked Falken.

"Once. Many years ago." His voice sounded cautious.

"What did you find?"

He touched one of the valleys. "This is the land of the
Equinox Women."

"Women?" Falken was wearing a grin.

"Women. Very fierce women who won't allow men
near their valley. Not even male children."

That sounded strange to Falken. "How do they
replenish their numbers?"

"They mate with any men that might be available, but
don't allow men in the valley."

"What about male children born to the women? All
the babies can't be female."

There was a strange note to Shona's voice as he
replied, "The male offspring are sacrificed."

Chapter
Six

★★★★★★★★

1700.

The three trains servicing AfriKorps had become a focal point of intrigue since their arrival on the continent. The trains had been shipped to Africa from the United States and were now deployed in three separate areas, giving the AfriKorps a 250 miles-per-hour rapid deployment capability into a combat zone.

Francine was the train servicing the north-south line to the edge of Quadrant One. Painted black, the solar-powered train was an awesome piece of machinery.

The engine was bullet shaped; on the sides were weapons platforms integrated into the hull. On the nose, another weapons system could pop out from its concealed station. The weapons were mostly rockets, with the exception of the nose system. The nose weapons platform was a 30mm six-barreled chain gun. The uranium-depleted bullets were armor piercing and could reduce a tank to scrap metal in an instant.

Trailing in tandem behind the main engine were several fortress cars, heavily armed platforms that provided flank protection to the train. Included in the string of railroad cars were a mess car and a hospital car where surgery could be performed.

The most impressive platform was called the hunter platform and it was armed with multiple-warhead image-seeking missiles. These were capable of being launched, seeking targets based on computerized images, and either killing the acquisitioned targets, or if none were found, returning to the launch platform where they could be recovered, rearmed if necessary, and redeployed.

From the ramps of other cars, infantry fighting vehicles could be loaded and deployed. More than a dozen cars were designed to deploy MBT's. Four cars were designated as the Armory.

The rear car was not a caboose, the traditional work car of the train. Instead, there was an exact replica of the front engine compartment, complete with weapons systems. The train could fight in either of two directions while putting out full fire suppression on the flanks from the inner platforms.

Creighton never ceased to be amazed by the train, initially called Iron Horse. Now that there were three, the trains were individually identified with their own names.

Hamp Floris was watching with satisfaction as the last of the crates holding the animals were loaded. Creighton and Puhaly were watching as well, both still reflecting their doubt with sullen faces.

TC pointed out what was common knowledge. "Hamp, I hope you've explained to your zoologists the threat that exists once we reach Quadrant Two. According to Armbrust there's a strong likelihood we will encounter hostile elements. As far as the animals are concerned, there's no guarantee they'll be safe. You could be providing nothing more than a helpless food source."

Hamp had a look that overflowed with confidence. "The animals will survive the hostiles. They've been raised in a biome, but they have a natural wariness for humans. They're not pets, TC."

Puhaly hawked and spit. "They look milk-fed and mommy-coddled to me." He pointed to a pair of giraffes. The roof of the car carrying the giraffes had been opened. The animals' heads stuck above the top of the car. "When the engineer hits 250 miles per hour, the resistance will blow their eyeballs out of their skulls. Or snap their necks."

Hamp chuckled, and as though on cue, he pointed at one of the train engineers. Forward of the giraffes, two men had begun installing a clear plastic windscreen that would protect the protruding necks and heads of the giraffes. "The windscreen will only lessen our speed by ten miles per hour. The giraffes will be perfectly comfortable."

Then the two soldiers heard a loud snort, and turned to see a vehicle approaching with two heavy crates.

"What the—" Puhaly stepped aside as the vehicle rolled past. He glanced into the side of the crate, which was enclosed with a heavy duty polymer glass, the type used to construct the biospheres and capable of withstanding a direct hit from a 120mm cannon.

The pair of white rhinos looked at the gunner aimlessly. Both were chewing a yellowish food mixture designed especially for rhinos.

"Butt ugly, aren't they, TC?" Puhaly laughed.

Creighton watched the animals as the vehicle stopped. He noticed that Eve was staring directly at him, and for a moment, felt a wave of enthusiasm for the project. "I think they're beautiful," Creighton replied. His voice was filled with awe. "I just hope you know what you're doing, Hamp."

"I do, TC, I do. This same project is now going on throughout the United States. In a few years, we'll be moving toward a better environment. Those decades of careful planning and technology in the biospheres will pay off. I just wish my father was alive to see this. He'd be proud."

Creighton remembered Hamp's father. Unlike the other "specials" in the biosphere, he hadn't been a soldier. He was known for his endless days of research in the various biomes, keeping alive animals that would one day be needed for replenishing the earth.

"He certainly would," TC replied, then he clapped Puhaly on the back. "Let's check on the squadron."

The two soldiers walked off as the forked arms of a heavy-duty lift gripped the crate holding Adam, then easily lifted the white rhino onto the deck of the transport car. When Adam was loaded, the clamshell door of the car sealed tight.

Hamp checked his watch. His voice nearly cracked as he said softly, "On schedule."

Chapter Seven

★★★★★★★

The one thousand mile journey began with nothing more than a low-frequency hum in the roundhouse where Frank Houser, the engineer, sat behind a computerized panel. On an overhead screen the track to the end of Quadrant One glowed evenly, a dark-blue line indicating the track was clear. At three intervals were red lights indicating substations, junctions along the track the train could use as repair facilities, or to offload equipment or personnel for the three outer defense perimeters forming the extended Iron Necklace of Quadrant One.

The defense lines ran from east to west, manned by pacified hostiles who were now trained and led by MNF personnel. Entire villages had sprung up within the defense positions, which could withstand any threat that might be thrown at the camps by the Marauders.

Even the track itself was fortified, capable of withstanding any type of demolition. Its computer could determine whether a particular part of the track was being serviced or tampered with. Heat sensors threaded through the track could differentiate between man or animal.

Houser punched in the command and the train eased out of the roundhouse, moving slowly along the track through the outer security fence surrounding Base Camp One.

Clayton was watching near the opening in the fence where the tracks were lit by high-intensity light. Beyond the fence the African desert was as black as the night.

The hum grew louder as the engine increased speed The cars began to pass and became a blur as the solar-driven engines pulled and pushed from fore and aft of the long procession.

When the animal cars appeared, he looked up to see the protective windscreen looming above the car carrying the giraffes. He saw two strange creatures, their skin yellow with black spots, and nearly laughed at them. But Clayton knew they had more of a place on the continent than he or the other humans.

Then, in a flash, the train was gone.

Chapter Eight

★★★★★★★

1900.

"Goddammit!" In the stockade, the security guard stared at the image of the prisoner on the television screen. Benhaddou lay on his side, motionless. His empty eyes were staring at the ceiling.

Following procedure, the guard picked up a telephone, punched in the number for the dispensary, then alerted the two guards sleeping in the next room. Then he alerted the officer of the day.

Ten minutes later, a medic arrived and followed the three guards and OD to the cell holding the Morocc. Benhaddou still lay on his side, not moving.

The medic watched as the three guards hoisted the prisoner to his cot and handcuffed his wrists and ankles to the frame. The medic couldn't hide the fact that he was nervous; the Morocc's viciousness was known throughout the military region.

"What's the disposition, doc?" asked the OD. He was a tall, muscular black man and kept a pistol levelled at the prisoner during the examination.

The medic shook his head. "He's gone into shock." The medic pointed at the three guards. "Get him over on his back."

The OD looked at him suspiciously. "Why?"

The medic replied, "I need to take his temperature. He's stiff as a board. I can't get a thermometer into his

33

mouth. I'll have to do it rectally." He tried to open the Morocc's mouth but the jaws were clamped tight.

The three guards removed the handcuffs and started to roll Benhaddou over onto his stomach. When the last steel cuff was off his ankle, and the prisoner free from the bed, his eyes opened.

The medic thought the eyes were filled with blood, but had little time to feel frightened. Benhaddou's powerful hands gripped his throat, and he felt his neck snap beneath the violent twist.

"Shoot!" ordered the OD, who stumbled backward automatically with sudden fright. The three guards fired, but the prisoner was shielded by the medic's body, which the Morocc held in the air like a rag doll.

A harsh kick from Benhaddou dropped one guard, crushing his chest. The second guard felt the medic slam against his body, sending him sprawling against the side of the cot where his head caved in. The third guard felt a vicious kick to the groin; the prisoner's foot seemed to fly up from between the medic's dangling legs.

"A-a-a-g-g-g-h-h-h!" The voice of Benhaddou raged as he drove the medic's body toward the OD. The officer was hit so hard his pistol flew from his hand.

The two living men pressed at each other from each side of the dead medic's body. Each man tried to exert his will in the life and death struggle they knew only one would survive. For a long moment both seemed suspended in the middle of the room, the pitiful face of the dead medic staring at the OD.

Like two great horned animals locked in combat, one waiting for the other to show a sign of weakening, the men groaned, grunted, and pushed with all their strength.

The battle was decided only when one chose to risk everything. With violent force, Benhaddou head-butted the back of the medic's skull with all his strength. The dead man's head slammed into the bridge of the OD's nose. Blood spurted, and in that split second, the OD weakened.

Benhaddou released his grip on the medic. The sudden weight of the body the OD now fully supported and the pain in his head left the opening Benhaddou had dreamed of for a year.

With a vicious punch to the throat, in the larynx, Benhaddou saw the OD's eyes bulge. The OD's hands went to his throat but were beaten to the same point by the massive hands of the prisoner.

Using all his strength, Benhaddou raised the OD from the floor and charged with all his might at the wall. The OD's back slammed violently; a sickening rush of air from his lungs washed over Benhaddou's face, and the Morocc knew he had won.

Benhaddou's fingers then closed around the throat of the OD and he watched as he squeezed the last breath of life from his captor's body.

Chapter Nine

★★★★★★★

Colonel Clayton had been in his office finalizing a report to the commission when the telephone rang. He strapped on his pistol and charged through the door, then drove to the stockade.

The front door of the stockade was being guarded by a pair of soldiers who saluted as Clayton entered the building. Inside, four other soldiers were at the security console, rewinding the videotape. On a separate television screen, Clayton could see the video projecting the activity inside the cell.

Soldiers were covering the bodies of the medic, the three guards, and the OD, who lay naked on the floor. Another soldier suddenly went to the sink and vomited.

"The tape's ready, sir," said one of the soldiers, who was ashen faced.

"Play the tape, son," Clayton ordered .

For five minutes Clayton sat and watched the scene unfold. He saw the guards enter, followed by the medic and OD. He shook his head as he saw their first fatal mistake. "You should have injected the room with the stun gas."

Clayton knew each cell was equipped with a non-lethal gas that renders the prisoner incapacitated for fifteen minutes. It was specifically designed to allow a thorough examination without the prisoner becoming injured by the effects.

When the videotape showed Benhaddou rising from the cot, Clayton felt the fear the medic must have experienced. Never had he seen such a violent exhibition of human strength. The guards were battered. Finally, there was the death struggle with the OD.

When the tape ended, the soldier sitting at the console looked weak. "Christ, sir. Did you see what he did to our men before he left the cell?"

Clayton took a telephone, talking as he punched in a number. "I saw it, son. It's his personal trademark."

"But their eyeballs, sir!" The young soldier nearly vomited. "He plucked out . . . then ate their eyeballs!"

Chapter
Ten

★★★★★★★

2000.

Aboard the train, Fergus Felot, the midgetlike driver of Creighton's MBT, Ribald's Chariot, was taking the brunt of the kidding. It was a usual occurrence. One that Felot often encouraged by his mere presence.

Puhaly looked at the squat man with the bearded face, and the gunner's nose pinched in distaste. "You smell pretty ripe, Fergus. When's the last time you had a shower?"

Fergus removed one of his boots and aimed a foot at Puhaly. His sock was nearly the color of the train. "Chew this."

Puhaly looked at TC. "I can hold his arms . . .but you have to grab his feet. We'll give the desert rat a bath. Otherwise, we'd be better off sleeping with those animals in the rear. I prefer their smell to Fergus's."

TC shook his head. "Not me. Fergus's feet are more deadly than a rattlesnake. I suggest we make him sleep with the animals."

"Not on your life,." Hamp Floris replied as he entered the car which carried Creighton's main battle tank. "Those animals are supposed to be nearing their mating season. Fergus's feet could alter the balance of nature."

"Shame on you selfish sonsabitches," Fergus snapped at TC and Puhaly, trying to act offended. "Now you're fucking with nature!"

Hamp's face settled into an angelic smile as he sat on the floor of the car. The hum of the train streaking over the tracks had a soothing effect on him. It was his first ride on the Iron Horse, and he found the movement exhilarating.

"What's with the zoologists?" asked Puhaly. "This fellow Sawyer is wrapped tighter than the core of a frag grenade. And the woman . . . Christ, she's so damn jumpy she makes me nervous."

Hamp looked away momentarily, as though searching for the right words. Finally, he tried to explain. Looking at Puhaly, he asked with dead seriousness, "Have you ever been frightened? I mean really frightened?"

Puhaly's gaze was steady as he answered without hesitation. "Not since I can remember. Why? Are they scared?"

"Terrified. This is their first journey out of the biosphere. They left their biospheres, boarded a train for the coast, then shipped to Africa with the animals. It's different for them. Different than what we were accustomed to. In the Western Quadrant of America we grew up with the hostiles. Their Quadrant was secured before they came out."

Puhaly shrugged. "Big deal. They have protection." He jerked his thumb at the Ribald's Chariot. "We could protect them from the Devil if necessary."

Hamp shook his head. "Not for long."

Puhaly was puzzled. "What do you mean?"

"The reserve will be off-limits to all military personnel. Which means . . . "

Before he could finish, Puhaly spoke for him. "Which means they'll be on their own."

"Completely. In order for the animals to regain their instincts for the wild, they must be given freedom from all human interference. Otherwise, they might not adapt. The attempt to introduce the animals back into their natural environment could be a total failure. In which case, they would consider it their failure. And that's the professional concern. Then there's the personal concern."

Puhaly was beginning to understand. "They might be victims of hostiles, or Marauders."

"Or the animals," Hamp added. "There's no way of predicting what the animals might do. The reserve must have total seclusion. No human violence can be tolerated."

"That presents another problem, Hamp." Creighton pointed out a weakness in the plan. "You might be able to keep our people out of the reserve. With patrols around the reserve you might be able to keep hostiles and Marauders out, though that will take some effort. But how do you keep the animals in the reserve? They might wander off. Animals don't exactly follow orders like humans."

Hamp's answer came immediately. "An electronic collar will be placed on each animal's neck. The collar will transmit data to the central computer at their station. The collar will also provide location, information pertaining to body vital signs, which will allow them to know when—and if—mating occurs. The collar on the female will indicate if pregnancy has occurred, and birth when the time is right. They will then track the female and collar the offspring."

"Fine," said TC. "But how do you keep them inside the reserve?"

"Once we reach the reserve, your first duty will be to set out a pattern of sensors around the area. Included in the collar is what they call a boundary influencer."

"What's a boundary influencer?" asked Fergus.

"The sensors are very high-powered. You will be setting them out in what will be three circular boundaries. This will create something similar to a force field. When a collar nears a sensor, the collar will emit a painful electronic shock. Like an electrical charge. Each animal is wearing a collar capable of emitting the proper amount of pain according to the type of animal. For example, you wouldn't put the same collar on the white rhino as on a small deer like the impala. The difference would be lethal."

TC could see how the collar could control the animal. "That keeps the animals in. Too bad you don't have something to keep the human element out. Will the sensors detect penetration from the outside?"

"Yes. Which explains the zoologists' apprehension. They are like children going outdoors for the first time. They're frightened, which is natural. But they're courageous. Don't ever doubt that."

Puhaly's lips pursed. His voice was tinged with admiration. "My apologies, Hamp. I had them figured for pansies. They're really ballsy, aren't they?"

"Quite," replied Hamp. He obviously admired the zoologists' courage. He recalled his first journey from the Vegas Biosphere to the outside. He was frightened, and he was surrounded by a squadron of fighting vehicles and battle tanks.

TC felt the train begin to slow. The hum diminished as the lessened off. He checked his watch. "We must be arriving at the substation."

The train drew to a halt. Puhaly had one final question as the clamshell door opened.

"Hamp, could we strap one of those collars on Fergus and put him in the reserve?"

Fergus threw his boot at Puhaly, and before Hamp could answer, the laughter was chilled as Reno and Shona entered the car looking grim.

Instinctively, TC knew something was terribly wrong. "What's happened?"

Chapter Eleven

★★★★★★★

"Perhaps I should have let you kill him last year." Shona's voice was soft as he spoke. "Had I not interfered, those men would be alive. And others might not be killed by my brother."

TC recalled trapping and crippling Benhaddou in the desert after the Morocc had slaughtered his wife. He wanted to kill the man, but Shona pleaded, not for Benhaddou's life, but for Creighton's salvation.

"If you kill him like this . . . you are no better than him."

Shona's words came echoing back as he thought of that night when he had held a knife to Benhaddou's throat. He shook his head. "You were right. What have you learned about his escape? Has he been found?"

"Colonel Clayton suspects he'll be moving south, through Quadrant One to find the Marauders or other hostiles he can trust," replied Reno Falken.

"That's a lot of territory to cover. More than 1,000 miles." TC tried to imagine infiltrating that vast expanse of controlled territory. "He'll be picked up somewhere along the line."

Shona didn't look convinced. "He has many disguises. Already he is dressed as one of your men. Benhaddou is like the desert, he can change shape before your eyes. We must be cautious."

Suddenly, TC looked at the nomad prophet. "Why do you say that?"

Reno looked at Shona. "Tell him."

Shona looked ashamed. His voice sounded shaky. "The camp was searched. They found nothing. Except one thing." He trailed off.

"Tell me, goddammit!" TC demanded. He felt himself trembling.

"Silver's grave," Reno said quickly, as though the words were too painful.

TC's eyes widened. "What about her grave!"

Shona put his hand on TC's shoulder. "Her grave was defiled. On the marker, what you call a tombstone, he had written your name . . . in his own blood." He appeared unable to say any more to his friend.

TC looked at Falken. "What else, Reno? There's more. What else!"

Reno took a deep breath and the words came out as the air rushed from his lungs. "Her body is missing. He took her body."

"Cocksucker!" Puhaly roared.

Creighton's eyes narrowed into two slits that seemed to nearly become lost in the hardened muscles of his face. His fists tightened and he felt the bile rise in his throat until he thought he would choke.

In that moment, all could see that there would be no quarter the next time the two men met. And they all knew that that day was inevitable.

For TC, the warning came back from beneath the crescent moon in the desert the night he had held a knife at Benhaddou's throat.

"If you kill him like this . . . you are no better than him."

But he no longer considered his salvation important. All he could feel was the rage.

★★★★★★★★★★★★★

PART TWO
WILDERNESS
SEA

★★★★★★★

★★★★★★★★★★★★★

Chapter
Twelve

★★★★★★★

1200.

Wilderness Sea was AfriKorps jargon for the point beginning at as the edge of the civilized part of the African continent.

End of track was also found on the banks of the Wilderness Sea.

To the south lay unpacified tribes of hostiles, nomads, and a regrouping army of Marauders. In devising his operational planning, Clayton had conceived the notion of extending the boundaries of AfriKorps by placing the security of the area under the authority of indigenous inhabitants who had been pacified and were now elements of the Iron Necklace operation.

Procedure dictated that when entering a particular area, the hostiles were to be approached through local intermediaries such as Shona, and convinced to become a part of AfriKorps. Diplomacy was stretched to its limits, and force used only if all other efforts failed, or the hostiles made overt physical threats against the AfriKorps.

Shona's task was simple: convince the hostiles their interests were best served by joining AfriKorps, which would offer food, medicine, clothing, and military training and equipment that would allow the tribes to protect their domain under the auspices of AfriKorps.

Once language barriers had been overcome, often through sign or symbol language, and the awesome array of AfriKorps firepower displayed, the indigents generally succumbed quickly.

However, first and foremost in the planning was the DR, or deep recon, the reconnaissance penetration by a squadron of MBT's with supporting IFV's. Contact could occur in the DR, and Clayton decided the DR should not be encumbered by the less swift and agile vehicles of the pacification teams.

The PT's followed in the rear, providing a hospital, water station, and commissary, among other things. The PT's were now staying close to the end of track, camped as additional security while waiting in reserve to assist the DR if necessary.

Captain Mike Armbrust, a muscular young officer with blue eyes, was a student of the ancient martial arts. He had been on DR for three months and was obviously tired as he waited for the arrival of Zada.

He was standing beneath a full moon, at the edge of the Wilderness Sea. Behind him, the end-of-track camp was quiet; guards patrolled the inner perimeter while IFV's circled the outer perimeter. At the core of the camp's defensive position, twenty-four main battle tanks, surrounded by other IFV's and their bivouacked troops, provided the power punch should an attack be launched.

Electronic mines lay beyond the perimeter between the inner core and the roving IFV's. Should Marauders or other intruders attack, there would be hell to pay.

Armbrust stepped up onto the roadbed and marvelled at the newest asset to the AfriKorps mission.

Unlike their predecessors of three centuries past, the work gang was not composed of graders, pick-and-shovelers, track layers, and spike drivers.

The process of raising and grading the bed, which rose four feet from the surface, laying crossties, then laying and joining track was done by one autonomous unit affectionately called "Roadbed Ruthie."

Ruthie was a large contraption that moved across the

surface, gouging up sand, which was conveyed through a heat compactor that literally turned the sand into liquid. The liquid sand was mixed with a rapid-cooling chemical, then channeled into the groove at the center of the machine.

Once the liquid was poured, the setting process followed almost instantly; however, before the cooling process was complete, crossties were implanted into the planed surface. The next step was the placement of interlocking tracks onto the ties.

Track was laid at the rate of five miles per hour. Track that would never have to be repaired. Like a giant snail leaves its slimy trail across the earth, Ruthie left her trail in the form of a continuous track of shiny rails.

Walking alongside Ruthie, Armbrust recalled talking with the track boss, who had explained the rapid deployment aspect of Ruthie.

"This machine can go anywhere except through water. She can cut through new territory at will with limited advance survey. Especially flat terrain, like the Eastern Quadrant."

"What about mountains?" He knew there were a lot of mountains to cross in the move south. He had already seen them, especially in the new region his squadron had finished reconning.

"We bring up prefabricated bridging that is made at Base Camp One in the roundhouse. Although the installation is actually slower than the grading and track laying, it can be done rather quickly and efficiently."

As a soldier, Armbrust had a greater concern than speed. "'What about sabotage?'"

The track boss had shook his head. "The roadbed is impervious to any type of conventional explosive. The bed is harder than steel once the sand is processed and compacted. The tracks can't be removed, so there's no chance of digging up the track."

"What about planting explosives on the track? The train could be blown off the track."

The track boss grinned. "The entire course of the tracks are threaded with thermal-imaging sensors. Tampering with the track will relay the exact location to the control center in the engine. The tracks can either be electrified—killing and clearing the track of intruders—or can identify the location, in which case the train is automatically stopped before reaching the detonating point."

"What about maintenance on the track?"

"We use what we call a pig. Anything goes wrong, we send the pig down the line. The pig carries a maintenance crew. Sand drifts are no problem, the engine has a modern version of a cowcatcher on the nose. We can plow through drifts thirty feet high at full speed. Fifty feet high at half speed. I don't believe drifts will get higher than that. If so, we'll find a way through."

Armbrust turned and looked down the track. Beneath his feet he felt a sudden hum against the soles of his boots. Seconds later, in the distance, he saw the powerful nose beacon flash on, the signal that the train was ten miles from the camp.

The signal to get off the track!

Chapter Thirteen

Having experienced his first ride aboard the Iron Horse, Shona stepped down from the main engine apparently impressed, and somewhat unsettled. Since the first meeting with AfriKorps, he had been constantly awed by the technology brought to the continent by the Americans and Europeans. But nothing had impressed him so thoroughly as the train, unless it was the presence of the animals that were to be reintroduced to Africa.

As a child, he had heard his mother recount the stories passed down to her by her father and grandfather, of the great animals that once roamed the earth in great abundance before the Cataclysm. In the year since the arrival of AfriKorps, he had begun to think there might be hope for the return of the good and great things to the continent.

But first, there was the evil to be dealt with. Which brought his thoughts again to Benhaddou. He knew without thinking what his brother was doing. Benhaddou would search for Creighton. And Shona knew this time there would be no quarter given by the young officer.

"Shona!" Armbrust came forward with his hand extended. They had served together on a Pac-Team in the last region of Quadrant One.

Armbrust touched the black patch on his right eye. The desert prophet could see that the man was recalling the day he and Creighton snatched Armbrust from the Marauders who had captured and tortured him, destroying his eye, as they had destroyed and slaughtered his platoon of MBT's.

"Congratulations, captain." Shona bowed slightly. "I understand you have been promoted."

Armbrust nodded, slightly embarrassed. "Where's TC?"

"Right here, young captain."

The two officers shook hands.

"Come with me." TC motioned for Armbrust to follow. "I'll show you your first priority."

Nearing the center of the train, Armbrust stopped in his tracks. He pointed at two heads looking about curiously from within an enclosed glass shield rising above one of the cars.

"What is that?" asked Armbrust.

"A giraffe," TC replied, pressing a small device that opened the side of the car forward of the giraffes.

The car opened. Armbrust and the African night were greeted by the sudden blast of a great roar.

"My God, TC, that's a lion."

"*Simba,*" Shona said almost reverently.

"How does Hamp figure to protect the other animals from this big fellow?"

"Quite simple, Captain Armbrust." The voice of Hamp Floris answered from inside the car. His head appeared, his pince-nez down on the end of his nose. "The lions will be segregated in their own part of the reserve, secured there by the sensors." Hamp explained the use of the sensors. "In a few years, they'll be allowed to mingle with the other animals. But not until there has been proliferation."

Armbrust shook his head. "I'd rather face a hostile with a sharp stick than that cat in the jungle. Look at those teeth."

The lion roared again and the sky seemed to shake.

"What will you feed them until that day comes?"

"The reserve will be stocked with a small herd of cattle for the sole purpose of being a food source."

"Cattle? I thought cattle were a taboo?"

Cattle, particularly flatulence from cattle, were known to have been one of the contributing factors to the greenhouse effect. That and the massive destruction of the earth's rain forests to provide more grazing ground for greedy international cattle barons.

One of the more ridiculous stories to survive pre-Cataclysm was the report that in 1991, the U.S. government gave Minnesota scientists over two million dollars in grant money to study the effect of cattle flatulence on the environment.

The Federal Fart Fund was the name often used to refer to the project.

Gases emanating from cattle rose into the atmosphere in the form of methane gas, and contributed significantly to the occurrence of the greenhouse effect.

"In limited numbers, captain," Hamp replied. "Cattle will be produced in limited numbers to serve as a temporary food source for certain species." He smiled. "We know what we're doing."

"I hope so." Armbrust sounded skeptical, and rightfully so. He looked at TC. "What's the game plan?"

"You'll stay here with the animals. I'll take my squadron into the Wilderness Sea to the site you found. We'll secure the area, and help set up the reserve. Then we push south."

A strange look crossed Armbrust's face. "It's strange down there, TC. Not like up north. Even the hills seemed to be haunted."

Shona's face hardened. "I have heard the stories of that area. Did you see any of the people? Especially a tribe of women?"

Armbrust shook his head. "No. But we found something that was strange."

"What?" TC was ready, as he had been before, to hear about anything that would keep him from being surprised or horrified.

"There's a place. . . . " His voice trailed off.

"What about this place?"

"Beyond the valley where the reserve will be located, there's another valley. It's surrounded by high ridges, but accessible. You'll see the route on my maps. We didn't find any sign of Marauder activity, but we did find evidence they had visited the valley on at least one occasion."

"What kind of evidence?" asked Creighton.

"Large burial pits and equipment that obviously belonged to the Marauders."

"The valley of the Equinox Women," Shona said somberly.

"Valley of the Damned would be a better name, TC."

"Why?"

"We found skeletons. Hundreds of skeletons. But no people."

"Why would that bother you, Mike? You've seen skeletons before."

"Skeletons, yes. But not where they were all children. That's what we found in one burial site. It was secluded from the others."

"Continue," Creighton ordered.

"Babies. Newborn, according to the medic. And they're all male."

Shona looked at Creighton. "Then it is true. The stories are true."

TC looked toward the vast darkness to the south, toward the Wilderness Sea. "We'll keep this to ourselves for the time being. I don't want my men psyched out by superstitious tales. Is that understood?"

They agreed.

Creighton clapped his hands together. "Come on. Let's get the equipment unloaded. I want to move out at daybreak."

Walking away with Armbrust and Hamp, Creighton realized Shona was missing. He looked back and saw the man standing by himself, staring toward the south.

It was the only time TC had ever seen the desert nomad show any sign of fear.

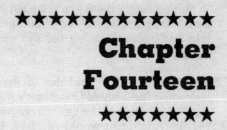

Chapter
Fourteen

★★★★★★★

1300.

The sentry at the security gate heard footsteps padding through the hot sand before he saw the figure approach from out of the shadows. Like most sentries, his concentration had been focused outward, toward the desert beyond Base Camp One.

Turning, he saw a tall man with a sand-covered uniform and face, as though he had been buried beneath the sand. That was the last thing he saw, except for the flash of the man's hand as the moon danced across the steel blade of a knife.

The blade pierced the sentry beneath the rib cage, then drove upward, severing the arteries of his heart. His knees buckled, and he fell lifeless into the arms of Benhaddou.

The Morocc pulled the sentry into the shadows where he had waited, then removed the dead soldier's webbing, field pack, and took his weapon.

Most important, he took the sentry's canteen. He recalled the map on the wall of the security guards' office in the stockade. He remembered the bright lights and the words denoting *substation*.

The first substation was a long journey. One that would require more than a canteen and strong legs. To reach the substation he would need the fuel of vengeance!

Sliding under the fence as he left Base Camp One, he nearly laughed as the sand warmed his neck. He had lain for hours, waiting for the chance to make his escape.

Not in the sand.

Above the sand. Sand that lay beneath the box that contained the body of Creighton's woman!

He had dug out the grave, removing the body, knowing the Americans would not look beneath the coffin. They would not look for a body still in the grave—buried beneath where he lay.

He had gambled none of the soldiers would notice the grave was not as deep as when it was initially dug.

He had lain there through the day and into the night, smelling her decaying flesh, listening to the enraged voices of the soldiers.

The voice he recalled most was that of the one called Clayton, who had judged him at the trial.

He had heard and understood Clayton when he had said that "Creighton's gone south. Thank God. He won't have to see this."

Minutes after sliding under the fence, Benhaddou began a steady jog through the desert, not concerned that he was leaving tracks in the sand. The wind was beginning to blow steadily from the north. His tracks would be covered and there would be no trace of which direction he was travelling.

Again, he was the hunter!

Chapter Fifteen

★★★★★★★

0500. End Of Track.

The Lion squadron rolled out in column formation, moving in near silence, except for the steady hum of the solar-powered engines of the MBT's. At the lead was Ribald's Chariot, TC Creighton's main battle tank.

The MBT, with treads made of ceramics, and protective outer "laser-shed" skin—an outer defensive mechanism that locked-up incoming artillery rounds by laser, then destroyed the projectile before impact—was stealth and "chameleon" capable. This meant that it was capable of reducing its thermal output to equal the outside temperature, and able to "paint" the outer shell the color of the environment. The Afrikorps MBT's were thus able to run silently, avoid thermal imaging, and remain nearly invisible.

A 120mm cannon jutted from the main turret, controlled by the gunner, who could select high explosive HEAT rounds, or armor-penetrating SABOT rounds. TIRT rockets could be launched from three platforms, sending a computer-guided image-response-tracking missile to the enemy tank. The tank's computer would lock-up the enemy tank tread, "wrap" the tread, and feed it into the computer memory, thus making the tank an integral part of the computer.

Accuracy was 100 percent.

Smoke canisters were on the outer hull, along with a

heavy 50-caliber machine gun near the tank commander's cupola. A 30mm cannon could be fired from one of the co-axial stations, as well as 7.62 light machine gun from another co-ax.

Thirty MBT's headed the column as it pushed south into the Wilderness Sea.

Twenty-four IFV's took up the flanks, their rubber tires boring smoothly through the desert. Each IFV was manned by a crew of two and carried eight infantrymen.

At the lead, TC gave his first command. "Reno, take the point. I want a ten-mile recon."

Falken took the point with four vehicles from the recon platoon. Racing forward, the recon vehicles were soon out of sight.

Looking back, Creighton could see the armada moving through the desert in smooth fashion. "Go to medium power," he ordered the column.

Nearly sixty rooster tails rose from the desert floor as the tanks and IFV's moved to medium power—forty miles per hour. The tanks took the terrain smoothly with barely a bump as the shock systems in their treads absorbed the desert seamlessly.

Standing at the end of track, Armbrust was watching the column through his field glasses as the last of the Lion squadron faded to the south, toward the Wilderness Sea. He lowered the glasses as a young soldier carrying a radio approached.

"Colonel Clayton's on the horn from Base Camp One."

Armbrust listened to the report, which was more like a warning, and wasn't surprised at what he heard.

"Be advised, the renegade and murderer Benhaddou has been reported moving in your direction."

Chapter Sixteen

★★★★★★★

0800.

Port Marrakesh was the oldest remnant of Morocco, and now sat on the edge of the Atlantic Ocean. After the Cataclysm, the rise of the ocean eroded the coastline when the polar icecaps began melting in the middle of the twenty-first century.

The harbor was protected by a battery of artillery, two dozen MBT's, and an infantry company. The fledgling United States Navy, once a powerful worldwide rapid deployment force, was now nothing more than a merchant fleet, whose task it was to transport vital supplies and equipment to the AfriKorps.

Captain Alissa Breen arrived with an anticipation she had never known before. Standing on the deck of the *Carolina,* a new SES, a hydrofoil surface-effect ship, she had watched the coastline come into view as the freighter approached the African coast.

What made the trip most unique was the fact she was alone—for the first time in her life, except for Dr. Shoemaker and his GroundStar personnel.

By 0800 Thunder One had been offloaded, placed onto a heavy tread-based lorry, and had begun the journey to the east. The desalinization plant lay to the south of the port. A highway stretched into the vast emptiness of the desert, in a line that appeared to disappear in the direction of a high mountain range.

For nearly a year she had heard reports of the AfriKorps, and couldn't help but wonder if a childhood friend might still be with the unit. She had spent part of her life growing up in the Vegas Biosphere, before her father was selected by President Dawson to become his chief of staff.

There were a few of her classmates she remembered, but one in particular came to mind: a handsome young man with dark hair and dark eyes. He was the one who had made her jealous of her best friend, whom she had learned had been killed while serving in Africa.

Reaching into her pocket, she removed a letter written to her by Silver Allenbey-Creighton on the eve of her departure from the United States. She had read the letter hundreds of times, always remembering the request made by her friend.

A request that should be fulfilled were Silver to die in Africa.

Chapter
Seventeen

★★★★★★★

0830.

Roman Standish was a stately gentleman who always wore a white toga, sandals, combed his long hair back, and tied it with a string. He was a philosopher and the teacher of many AfriKorps soldiers, especially those from the Vegas Biosphere where he was born and lived before coming to Africa.

Africa.

The name had mystified him when he was first approached to join the AfriKorps expedition as the unit negotiator. Schooled in reason, it was assumed he would be valuable at the right time and place. On many occasions he had been: in the desert when he had first met Shona, Roman had soothed the tortured souls of soldiers who had seen and done too much to other men.

Now he was tired. Perhaps, he thought, it was time to return to the desert of the western United States and fulfill his lifelong desire to journey from biosphere to biosphere, engaging other philosophers who were searching for the answers that might explain the past century of horror. He was tired of the bloodshed.

Knocking on Colonel Clayton's office door, the teacher waited for admittance by the former student. He entered to the refreshing chill of the air conditioning. The heat had always tortured Roman; unlike the others, who seemed to thrive on the heat as though they were desert reptiles, he often wished he had been born in the Arctic.

Colonel Clayton dropped a single sheet of paper onto the desk. He looked at it, then slowly scanned the words until he came to the scrawled signature of Roman Standish.

"Request denied," Clayton said in a voice that was neither cruel nor overjoyed. It was obvious to Roman that the commander had given his request for return to the United States great consideration.

"May I ask why?" He needed to know, though he knew it would not make a difference. Clayton was a man who never rescinded an order, nor gave explanation for his decision.

The commander waved a hand at the philosopher, as though he were taking valuable time.

"We need you, Roman. It's that simple."

Standish shook his head and pressed for a reason. "That's not an adequate answer. Please explain."

"There's a great deal of work for you here. Why do you want to return to the United States? There's nothing there but the drudgery of life. Here—there are challenges. Challenges that require men such as yourself to help us understand the people we're dealing with. Dammit! Can't you see this is different than America. In America we were pacifying our own country. Here, we're trying to rebuild society with the people who own the continent. We need your mind. Your understanding." Clayton paused, as though lost for the right word.

Sensing the word, Roman said, "My compassion?"

"Compassion! Hell, yes! Compassion." He seemed embarrassed to deal with such a notion.

Roman stood and walked to the window. Outside he could see a column of transport lorries enter the camp through the main gate. "They keep coming. Always something new. Some new dimension of destruction. The young men and women, many of whom won't return."

"Christ! Roman, you're starting to sound maudlin."

"Maudlin? Perhaps. But I'm tired of the destruction.

Tired of not seeing anything new blossom in this world except headstones above the bodies of our young."

Clayton sat back in his chair. He reached into his drawer. "Remember Dr. Eliason?"

Roman nodded. Dr. Carl Eliason and hundreds of other Americans had been discovered months before in a deep pyramid-shaped survival crypt in the Sahra desert, once called the Sahara. The Americans were cryogenically preserved for the long period of the Cataclysm, then rose from the desert like the phoenix from its ashes.

"Certainly." He saw Clayton holding a glass bottle.

"This is scotch." He pulled on a cork that sealed the bottle. "Eliason had a wine cellar in the pyramid. He left me a case of this stuff. It'll make your eyes roll, but it's soothing in times of stress. And in times of uncertainty."

Clayton poured and offered a glass to Roman. The philosopher took a drink. His face skewed up, then he smiled as the one-hundred-year-old scotch whiskey hit his system.

"Delightful."

Clayton drained his glass and leaned forward on his elbows. He steepled his fingers, then began talking very carefully. "I'm willing to grant you your request, Roman. But first, there's something I need for you to do. It's a personal matter. One I've been intending to address for several years. Frankly, I don't know how. I figured you might be the answer."

Roman looked at the bottle, which was labelled Aberlour, and motioned his glass toward the scotch. "Pour us another, then tell me your problem."

An hour later, Roman Standish walked unsteadily from the commander's office. He wasn't certain if his lack of equilibrium was caused by the scotch, or by Colonel Clayton's revelation.

For the first time in his life, Roman Standish wasn't certain how he would handle a matter so delicate it could cause the destruction of one—or possibly two— men he admired and respected.

Chapter Eighteen

1200.

Captain Breen had spent the morning preparing Thunder One for its maiden flight over Africa. When ready, she started the solar-powered engines and eased the throttle forward. As the aircraft moved ahead she felt the bumpiness, and realized that since she would be flying in and out of areas not equipped with concrete runways, the landing gear would have to be reinforced as soon as possible.

The nose came up and she saw the vast openness of the desert to the east. Taking a heading for Base Camp One, she saw the outline of the Atlas Mountains and felt the thrill of being the first woman to fly over Africa since the Cataclysm.

Thunder One was not armed with weaponry, but she had read the briefing and her orders which would direct her through pacified territory. There was nothing in her path to fear in the way of enemy activity. She settled back in the seat and made the one-hour flight to Base Camp One.

Chapter Nineteen

Colonel Clayton was waiting at the blacktop road designated as the runway that would receive Thunder One. On seeing the aircraft approach, he felt a wave of exhilaration. What he had planned for Thunder One would begin immediately, if the pilot was everything the personnel file had indicated.

Breen landed the aircraft smoothly and taxied to where she saw Colonel Clayton standing. She switched off the engines, opened the canopy, and stepped onto the runway. She saluted, then removed her helmet.

Clayton's jaw dropped as he saw the long hair spill onto her shoulders. "I didn't realize you were a woman."

She slipped the helmet under her arm and motioned to the aircraft. "How about a grand tour, colonel?"

Clayton liked her immediately. She seemed direct and unapologetic. After explaining the overall situation, and pointing out her role in the establishment of GroundStar, Clayton asked, "How soon will you be prepared to begin operating in this theater?"

She didn't have to think to reply. "I've been aboard that ship for longer than I care to remember. Frankly, I'd like to begin immediately. Thunder One is ready to fly. I'd prefer my mission to begin as soon as possible."

Clayton examined her. He knew the best way to test a new concepts—or people—arriving in Africa was to throw them immediately into the fire. They would be tempered—or melt under the heat.

"How about today? You can fly downrange to the end of track, stay overnight, then join our advance element in Quadrant Two. They could use your aircraft for aerial observation."

She nodded. "That's what I came here for. When will the GroundStar personnel follow?"

"Directly," he replied, then motioned toward a Landrover. "But first . . . you must be hungry."

She shook her head. "No. I'm too excited to eat. But there is something I'd like to do. It's of a personal nature."

"What's that?"

"I'd like to visit the cemetary. A friend of mine is buried there. Captain Silver Allenbey-Creighton."

Colonel Clayton felt a tightness in his stomach, and knew that it was time that he, too, addressed a personal matter.

"I'll drive you, Captain Breen."

Chapter Twenty

1400.
Creighton stood at the edge of the Wilderness Sea. To the south lay hills and deep savannah grasslands that spread inland to the base of a mountainous region that ran from east to west.

"It's beautiful." The voice of Dr. Jean Peterson sounded awestruck.

Creighton rolled up the sleeves of his desert fatigues. The sun was hot, giving the green foliage to the south a shiny appearance. "Beautiful . . . but deadly." Creighton motioned to Falken, who was standing by his IFV.

"I want you to recon the area to the front. Use two teams . . . each team composed of two IFV's and one MBT. Hold the MBT's in reserve in case of trouble. You know what to watch for. Report anything unusual. Take Shona with you."

Reno left with the two recon teams. One team went to the west, the other to the south. The two teams would work the area from outside to inside, clearing a corridor for the column to follow.

Turning to Jean Peterson, Creighton saw that the two zoologists were standing alone beside his MBT, wearing the look of the abandoned. "Dr. Peterson, you and Dr. Sawyer will transfer to another IFV." Creighton made a pumping motion with his arm. An IFV rolled up and the rear door opened, revealing eight soldiers sitting in their harness seats that lined the hull.

Peterson started to get inside the IFV, then came over to Creighton.

"Are you expecting trouble?"

"I'm always expecting trouble. The recon teams will make certain there's no ambush. At the same time they'll scout the best trail into the valley."

Creighton raised the binoculars to his eyes and studied the southern wall of the first valley. A momentary look of concern registered on his face as he slowly scanned the valley selected for the reserve.

"Is there something wrong?" She couldn't help but notice the muscles tightening around his mouth.

Creighton lowered the binoculars and looked at the woman. She looked frightened and out of place. She was biosphere-raised in a region that had been cleared of hostiles before she was old enough to know the danger that once loomed around the protective glass shelters.

TC understood, and he tried to allay her fears with a soft smile. "Nothing we can't handle." He trained the binoculars on the valley. "Would you care to see your new home?"

A wave of exhilaration swept through her as she saw the valley that would be the reserve. Then she tensed as she saw something else. "Is that what I think it is?" She was pointing to the west end of the mountains forming the northern wall of the valley.

"It could be," Creighton replied tersely.

She raised the binoculars again; she wasn't looking at the mountains, nor the lush savannah grasslands.

She was looking at a single pillar of smoke rising from the valley.

Chapter
Twenty-one

★★★★★★★

In the valley where the old man lived, Ibo squatted on a ridge facing north. A narrow tunnel, formed by erosion, led from his cave to the ridgeline where he could see the entire flatlands of the north, and the savannah to the west. It was where he began and ended his day, perched like some great bird, watching for signs of trespass or danger.

In his hand he carried the strange club with the metal shaft. As he rolled it with his fingers, Ibo watched the club's head flip from side to side, and he pondered the sight to the north.

Strange vehicles approached cautiously; a column from what he could see. These vehicles were much larger, and more sophisticated than those of the intruders that he had seen arriving from the south on many occasions.

Slipping back into the cave, he sat for a long while, thinking about what course of action he would take. He was an old man, no longer strong enough to fight for his valley.

Ibo reached a decision. One he realized he had been forced to reach on many occasions over the decades.

He would hide.

Chapter Twenty-two

★★★★★★★★

1430.

The recon column sat at the mouth of the first valley. All units seemed to be waiting for the order from Reno Falken. The sky was brilliant; white as burning steel. There wasn't the slightest trace of wind. Not a sound was heard over the supersensitive sound receptors on the IFV. That wasn't unusual; however, something else was, and that gave reason to pause and be cautious.

Reno Falken, though young, was an experienced soldier who relied on instinct when uncertainty existed. Instinct, he knew, had saved him on more than one occasion, helping him make split-second decisions when his brain was too slow to process information. Or when there wasn't enough information. That was the case as he sat in the commander's chair of his IFV, studying the imaging screen mounted on the console. The IFV's thermal-imaging camera swept a full 360 degrees from the roof mount, separating various heat sources into specific shades of color. The sky appeared white; terrain a soft green. Should a human image appear, the sensors would depict it as a red target, exactly like the one he was watching move through the underbrush roaming upward from the base of the valley toward a ridgeline.

Using the designation code—the Lion Squadron's recon team was named Fireball—he sent two units into the valley. "Fireball One . . . proceed at slow advance.

Take Shona with you. Fireball Two . . . follow in support. Maintain surveillance on the right front. Imaging reads a target at 300 meters. Human. On foot. A solo target."

Shona emerged from one of the IFV's and went to the lead MBT. He climbed inside Fireball One, then the two main battle tanks eased forward, their engines purring as the solar skin pumped energy to the main drive shaft.

A thin cloud of dust rose, then the tanks seemed to disappear and become part of it as the tank commanders went to chameleon mode, the cloaking countermeasure tactic that could literally make the tanks invisible.

Reno opened the cupola of the IFV and slipped on the harness of the 7.62mm machine gun mounted in the gun turret.

Keying the mike, he waited until the MBT's were downrange 200 meters, then ordered the trailing IFV commanders, "Saddle up the ground elements. The forward block is nearly in position. Ground element prepare to sweep from east to west."

From the IFV's, the whirr of the rear ramps opening signalled the ground troops to prepare for debarkation.

Once the ramps were opened, helmeted infantry troops double-timed from the rear of the IFV's, alternately moving right and left.

Three hundred meters ahead, the two MBT's slowed, then swung on-line, facing the southern wall of the valley.

Glancing down into the IFV, Reno could see the imaging screen. The red thermal image was stationary.

Reno keyed the mike. "Shona. Check out the target. Target is approximately 200 feet up the ridgeline from the base. Ground elements . . . prepare to provide suppressive cover fire."

Shona walked toward the inclining terrain; in his hand he carried a long spear. The caution the man exercised as he carefully worked his way through the rocks added to the tension. At one point he disappeared from

Reno's line of sight. When he finally reappeared, Falken wiped at a stream of sweat running from his forehead.

"Nice and easy, Shona. You're almost on the target," Falken whispered at the nomad.

Suddenly, Shona stopped. He knelt and ran his hand over the ground. In the next instant, from the corner of his eye, he caught the movement of a shadow emerging from the underbrush. Looking up, he saw a tall figure framed against the hot sun as it lunged at him with cat-like quickness.

His mind registered the fact that he was being attacked and that the attacker was no ordinary adversary.

Neshu, the leader of the Equinox Women, had chosen to attack, securing the advantage, rather than waiting to be discovered.

How, she asked herself, could she have been spotted? She had stayed in the underbrush, watching the strange vehicles approach. She had not moved, except slightly, to inch forward the spear she was now thrusting at the black man who stared at her with surprise, but not fear.

Her spear came down toward his head. Shona stepped inside the line of attack, raising his spear to parry the blow. The report of the two weapons making contact rang through the stillness.

He rotated his spear 180 degrees, a whirling move that threw the attacking spear outward from Neshu's body.

He saw a weak spot exposed at her belly. A quick side slash from the end of Shona's spear caught Neshu in the belly. He could feel the hardness of her muscles as the spear seemed to bounce off her flesh.

She grunted, then swung her spear again, this time at his knees. The heavy wood found purchase at the kneecap. Another sharp crack rang out.

Shona grunted, but still on his feet, stepped forward with his right leg, extending his body downward. He planted a hand on the ground, then fired out both feet, catching Neshu in the breasts.

Neshu flipped straight backward, falling on her shoulders. Shona saw her eyes glaze, then loll.

He didn't give her a chance to recover. Driving the spear point at her throat, he stopped it there, touching but not piercing the skin.

For a long moment their eyes were joined in mutual distrust. She started to move, then relaxed as the spear point pressed against her larynx.

"Where are the others in your tribe?" Shona's voice hissed.

Neshu shook her head. She didn't understand.

Shona spoke to her in another language. This time she understood.

Slowly, she lifted herself to her knees. Her breasts were exposed, momentarily averting Shona's attention.

Again he snapped his question.

"In the next valley. They've been taken captive by strangers from the south. Strangers with white skin."

Chapter
Twenty-three

★★★★★★★

Reno Falken had been momentarily numbed by the attack, one he had not anticipated in the wake of the overpowering numerical superiority of his forces. "Damn." Reno spit, then ordered the ground troops, "Move out. He's in trouble!"

Infantry troops charged up the hillside and the co-axials from the MBT's trained on Shona and the woman. The first soldier to reach Shona saw the nomad raise his hand, indicating there was nothing to fear.

Falken climbed out of the IFV and made his way to Shona, who was leading the woman down the incline. His strong hand gripped her by both wrists. The first impression Falken had of Neshu was the intense hatred burning in her eyes.

"Jesus," he said to Shona. "She looks like she would like to cut out my heart and eat it for lunch."

"She would," Shona replied.

"Where does she come from?"

"She is one of the Equinox Women. They hate men. Especially white men." There was no subtleness in his warning.

Reno shrugged, then went to the IFV. He reported to Creighton. "We have a prisoner. A nasty bitch that looks like she needs a good meal. There's something else . . . she told Shona there's white men in the next valley."

Creighton responded, "Return to my position.

Maintain two MBT's for a listening post."

Reno gave the orders. "Put her in my IFV." Minutes later, as the column returned to the main element, he regretted that decision.

The stench from her body was nearly unbearable.

Chapter
Twenty-four

★★★★★★★

Major Vita Slazenger was short, stocky, with blonde hair and green eyes. Her sloe-eyed gaze masked a determination that was no secret to the men in the armored column she was commanding. The daughter of a colonel who had died two years before while stopping a conspiracy of officers from overthrowing the government, she had been given an armored command as a reward for her dead father's loyalty.

She could have cared less for her father; but his death served her purpose. It was no secret she took every opportunity to prove she was as capable as any male officer—and as ruthless. A point she was preparing to make.

Her army was facing a new enemy that had joined the Europeans to halt the Marauder nations' designs on the farmland of Europe. Intelligence reports had confirmed the new arrival as AfriKorp, composed of European forces supported by soldiers from America.

She had read about America while growing up in the biosphere, and had known one of the Marauder tank commanders killed in combat with the AfriKorps on the eastern flank of the Northern Quadrant. The Marauder division had been sent to the eastern flank to launch a surprise attack against the less-advanced forces from Europe.

Good tactic—wrong enemy. Which was why she was

in the area at this moment. The arrival of the new troops, with superior technology and the intent to pacify the tribes and use them against the Marauders, had forced the strategists to reassess their plan.

The old plan was scrapped. An open battle with the AfriKorps would be suicide. A new plan was devised, one that would deprive the AfriKorps of its technology. The plan was simple: strike the Americans and Europeans at what historically had been their greatest weakness—conscience.

Conscience was an unknown concept to Slazenger, one she was not trying to learn, but rather, to understand.

"Bring the women and the children," Slazenger ordered some of her troops.

Soldiers began searching the huts which were made of thatch, another noticeably distinct difference from other tribal villages. Most of those she and her troops had razed had been made of mud, or were nothing but caves carved into the sides of hills.

Within minutes, twenty women and nearly a dozen children were lined up facing a squadron of tanks. There was no whimpering or crying from the captives; they faced their captors with glaring eyes, and mouths tight with hatred.

Slazenger strode forward, pulling a black man the women had kept imprisoned in one of the huts. The man was emaciated; the bones in his chest nearly pressed through his skin. His face was gaunt; his eyes sunken and hollow. He looked as though he had been held captive for a long period of time. But she knew that wasn't the case.

Slazenger pointed at the Equinox Women and children. "Are these the ones who slaughtered my men?"

The black man spit at the women. It was his only gesture. He nearly fell as Slazenger pushed him away. She turned and addressed the captives.

"You murdered my men. For that you will pay." She

raised her arm.

A chilling metallic clatter filled the air as her soldiers cocked their weapons. From the tanks, co-axial machine guns took aim from the turrets.

"Fire!" Her arm dropped.

Like rag dolls caught in a tempest, the women were swept from their feet, thrown backward by the wall of cutting, slicing steel spitting from the barrels of the Marauder weapons.

In the center of the village, a cacophony rose from the bodies of the twisting, shrieking captives, then their voices were lost in the tornado of noise from the machine guns.

Moments passed, then there was silence, except for the moan of a child nearly severed at the waist.

Her moan was silenced as Slazenger's pistol roared.

Chapter Twenty-five

Creighton didn't need an explanation. The sound that resembled thunder had clearly come from the south. Now there was silence. Then he heard the voice of the tank commander in the first valley.

"Fireball One to Lion command. Request permission to proceed to next valley."

Creighton looked at his map on a fold-out map stand and noticed the terrain separating the two valleys. "Negative Fireball One. Return to column. Avoid contact."

Creighton was well aware of the AfriKorps' worst nightmare: the possibility that one of the MBT's might be captured by a Marauder attack, allowing the enemy to study the technology, or worse, copy it. It was considered militarily essential that the MBT's be kept from the enemy, otherwise, the superior numbers of the Marauders would be overwhelming. The enemy from the south had proven its ability to learn new techniques; the results would undoubtedly prove disastrous.

Creighton left the map stand and marched to where a shower stall was being used. A square stall stood upright with water feeding from a water bag through a hose that ended in a shower nozzle at the top of the stall. A steady stream of water was pouring into the enclosed stall.

"How much time does she need?" Creighton asked in a voice that was somewhat astonished. The Equinox

Woman had been in the shower for nearly a half-hour.

Shona shrugged, then grinned. "I think it is the first time she has enjoyed such a luxury."

Puhaly was standing guard at the shower stall with Shona. The gunner grumped, "She'll need another hour to get the dirt off, TC. That's the dirtiest woman I've ever seen."

"She doesn't have an hour. We need to talk. Get her out." He pointed at the stall.

Puhaly grinned as he opened the stall. Then he was sent flying backward as a long leg extended from inside, the foot striking the gunner in the stomach.

Laughter erupted inside the camp. Puhaly started toward the shower again, but stopped at the voice of Dr. Peterson. She approached the stall calmly, but with caution. In her outstretched hand she held a towel for Neshu. The woman's long slender arm extended from the stall.

"Who ever heard of a bloody hostile being modest?" asked Fergus.

Shona shook his head. "She's not modest. You must remember . . . the Equinox Women hate men. They use them only to service the reproductive need."

"Far as I'm concerned they can fuck themselves!" Puhaly snapped.

Neshu stepped from the shower; her long braids dripped beads of water. The towel was wound around her body, covering her from the top of her breasts to just above her knees. Her face was now softer looking, thought Shona, suddenly noticing the remarkable facial features of the woman.

"Let me handle this, gentlemen." Jean approached the woman cautiously, but obviously unafraid. In a friendly gesture, she extended her hand to Neshu. After staring at the hand for a long moment, she gripped Jean's fingers and followed as she was led to where a tent had been erected.

The men stood dumbfounded, looking at each other

curiously. After thirty minutes, Jean and Neshu came out of the tent. A low whistle was heard from one of the soldiers.

"Jesus." Puhaly gasped. "Would you look at that."

"I've heard of making a silk purse out of a sow's ear . . . but I've never seen it happen."

"Hold your horny horses, Fergus," Puhaly mumbled. "Pretty or not . . . she kicks like a mule."

Shona's mouth parted in a slight smile as his eyes studied the woman. "Beautiful."

Neshu walked proud and erect, obviously feeling the effect of her transformation. She wore a desert fatigue jacket and shorts; her hair was combed back, wound into a bun on her head. Her lips were red with lipstick supplied by Jean Peterson. Her cheeks glowed slightly from rouge.

Jean Peterson appeared pleased. Impressed with the Equinox Woman's appearance, Creighton walked to the zoologist's side.

"You should have been a diplomat," TC whispered.

Jean smiled. "The Cataclysm robbed the earth of many things, captain. But I doubt there's any calamity that can strip women of their entire dignity in a mere century. And she is beautiful."

Shona approached and bowed slightly. Without ceremony he opened his robe, revealing scars on his chest.

"What is he doing?" Jean whispered to Creighton.

"Exchanging credentials. Shona is a chief. Chiefs wear scars on their chests to impress other chiefs."

Neshu fumbled with the buttons on the blouse, then revealed her breasts to Shona.

"Look at those bazooms," Fergus breathed heavily.

Puhaly pointed. "Look at those scars."

Neshu had tiny scars in the cleavage of her breasts.

The two chiefs walked away together and spoke for several minutes. When they returned to the AfriKorps soldiers, Neshu appeared less hostile.

"What did she tell you, Shona?" asked Creighton.

Shona sat in the sand, and as though asked, Neshu sat across from him. Shona began to explain what he had learned.

"The woman's name is Neshu. She is chief of the Equinox tribe. The tribe is composed of women. No males, except children, and they are not kept after birth."

Creighton's features twisted into a look of incredulity. "You mean, they . . ."

Shona nodded mournfully. "I do not try to understand. I am only telling you what I've learned."

Creighton swallowed hard. He had seen too much in his young life to be surprised; but that didn't mean he had to like what he had seen. "Go ahead. Finish your report."

"Last month the village was entered by white men in tanks. Men with blonde hair, blue eyes, much like your men. It was the time of the year when day and night share the earth for the same time period."

"There are two such periods. Six months apart. Vernal and autumnal equinox," Creighton interrupted. "One in spring, the other in fall. It's now fall."

"The men joined in the ritual of the mating rite, which the women of the Equinox have twice a year to replenish their population. Once the mating was over, the women killed the men." He shrugged. "It is their way."

"Jesus. Sounds like a black widow spider," Creighton said acidly. He looked at the woman. "She doesn't look that fiendish."

"She is not fiendish. She is doing what she was taught to do from childhood. Like other tragedies, the customs of her tribe have been shaped by the Cataclysm."

"Why do they have this custom?"

"In the past, their ancestors were enslaved and devoured by other tribes. These tribes were dominated by men. Fifty years ago the women escaped and formed their own tribe. They became fierce warriors. Feared in this land. The stories travelled as far north as my tribe."

"So they don't like men. Fine. What about the Marauders? How many were there?"

"Thirty. All dead. Killed at the end of the ritual. Except for the man that brought the Marauders to the Equinox valley."

"Why didn't they kill him?"

Shona looked at Neshu. "The Equinox Women make a sacrifice to the newborn on the day the last child is born from the previous mating."

Creighton felt a chill run down his spine. "What was she doing when we captured her?"

"Hunting for food. Berries. Plants. Small animals."

Creighton thought of another question. "Will her people attack the zoologists who are here to establish the reserve?"

"I don't know. But it's doubtful. You have many men. She is no fool. She will see you could destroy her village with your weapons."

Creighton recalled the sound of thunder coming from the other side of the valley. "You heard the noise from the valley where her village is located?"

Shona nodded. "She was in the shower. She did not hear the sound."

"You know what that probably means."

There was sadness in Shona's voice. "The Marauders have returned to the village."

Creighton stood and motioned to Falken. "Saddle up. We're going into the valley of the Equinox tribe."

2000.

The sun was settling to the west twenty minutes after the column had entered the valley that lay to the south of the one selected for the reserve. Creighton was impressed with the foliage, which was thicker, more lush than the barren sand dunes and hot deserts of the northern part of the continent.

Trees were small, mostly shrub, but he could see that somehow nature had retained its ability to regenerate the fauna and flora despite the devastation of the Cataclysm. In a sense, nature had survived better than man, which he figured was fitting, since it was man who had brought about the Cataclysm.

Surprisingly, by studying the carpeting of foliage flowing east, he had determined earlier that larger trees were probably growing in the valley's interior. It would be a perfect area for the reserve.

The Equinox village was reached an hour later. Night had fallen. Sounds were nonexistent, except the steady hum of the solar engines.

Falken was moving ahead with the two Fireball units and four IFV's, providing recon for the advance. The column was in a staggered formation, moving at echelon left with Ribald's Chariot at the lead.

Puhaly had the 120mm cannon locked and loaded with a high-explosive HEAT round. Riding buttoned up,

Creighton was in his commander's chair, watching the thermal imaging screen.

The terrain offered little resistance to the tanks which plowed through the underbrush with expected ease. The advance was going along smoothly, until the voice of Falken buzzed over the radio.

"We're on the outskirts of what appears to be a village, TC."

"What do you have, Reno?" Creighton replied.

Through his night vision device Falken could see the village lay quiet. There were no fires. "Nothing on visual."

"What about sound?"

"Checking for sound." Falken switched on the sound intensifier receiver, which could detect noise from 1200 meters away and amplify it. The reading indicator was showing a faint sound.

"Getting a slight reading from the village. Nothing heavy. It appears to be vacant of life and equipment."

"Hold your position. We're en route." Reno sat back in his chair. Looking into the interior of the IFV, he saw the concern in Shona's face. The woman sat beside him. She appeared to be made of stone.

Falken shook his head slightly at Shona. There was more said in that gesture than any words Falken might have spoken.

Reno turned back to the night vision scanner. He slowly scanned the village while listening to the sound intensifier. There was something out there, but what? Animal? A child crying? He wasn't certain. That was when he picked up movement on the scanner.

Falken could make out the image of something moving through the village. The figure was upright, eliminating the possibility of an animal. Zooming the telescopic lens, the figure appeared to sway while moving.

"We've got something moving in the village," Falken said to Shona.

Shona slid beside him and studied the movement.

"It's one of the women," he whispered.

Falken looked at him seriously. "You heard that gun-fire. Marauders don't leave survivors."

"A Marauder?"

Falken eased to the rear of the IFV and pressed the switch that lowered the ramp. He looked at Shona as he took an automatic rifle. "Let's find out."

The two men slipped down the rear ramp and disappeared into the darkness.

Chapter
Twenty-seven

Through his night vision goggles, Falken could read the ground perfectly. The tracks from tank treads had cut grooves in circular patterns. There were dozens of circles, except where the tanks had turned sharply, the driver braking the tread on one side of the tank, lurching the machine in that direction. The circles wound around the thatch hut village, finally tightening until the huts had been crushed beneath the massive treads.

The bodies lay spread-eagled in the dirt; some were crushed, though Falken could see all had been shot first. Most were women; a few children. There was no sign of life.

Shona reached and gripped Falken's shoulder. The strength in the nomad's hand turned Falken toward a crushed hut, where, in the green field of the night vision goggles, Falken could see something sitting on the ground.

Bent low, Falken and Shona slipped silently across the hard ground, shadows among shadows until they reached the figure sitting on the ground.

Ibo was caught by surprise. He yelped as Falken grabbed one arm, Shona the other. The old man was ripped to his feet as though the men had jointly raised a feather.

"Who are you!" Falken hissed in the man's ear.

There was the sound of a weapon cocking. The old man didn't recognize the sound; he had never seen weapons before, except the clubs and spears of the Equinox Women.

He did understand the cool metal pressing against the bottom of his chin. Through the pale moonlight he saw the strange goggles worn by the men, felt the cold barrel, and knew it was useless to fight against them.

He could only tremble.

His club was in his hand, but he didn't try to fight. That was useless; besides, his arms were drained of strength by the powerful grips.

Ibo mumbled something Shona thought he understood.

Mefendi.

"What did he say?" Falken asked.

"He said . . . 'friend.' I have not heard this language spoken in many years."

"Can you speak the language?"

Shona answered by asking Ibo, "Where do you come from, old man?"

Ibo looked astonished, as Shona watched through the green field of the night vision goggles, waiting for the answer that finally came in a weak voice.

"From the other valley."

Shona translated.

"Are there more like him?"

Shona asked and received the answer. "He is alone."

Falken took the mike from his portable short-range radio. "TC . . . we've found one old man. He's not one of the Equinox. But he sure as hell is scared. He might have seen what happened, though it doesn't take much imagination to figure that out. They're all dead."

Ibo watched Falken and thought the young man insane. He was talking into his hand, as Ibo had often talked to his stick.

Was he also insane?

There was a pause, then Creighton's voice cut through the night. The old man jumped as he heard Creighton's reply and thought he was hearing a strange voice from the dead.

"Hold your position. We're en route. Out."

Falken clipped the hand mike to his harness. He took a flashlight and turned on the beam, lighting the old man's face.

Ibo jumped as though struck by lightning, which was what he thought he was seeing, only this lightning stayed constant, shining in his eyes, blinding him.

"God . . . he must be a thousand years old," Falken said with astonishment.

Shona chuckled. "He is one of the few old ones who have survived many years."

Falken thought for a moment. "Through the Cataclysm?"

Shona replied, "I have seen many strange things since birth." He took his flashlight and pointed at the old man's hands. His skin was wrinkled; his knuckles stuck out like rocks lying on the ground. In his fist he gripped a club with a shiny shaft topped with a wooden head.

Shona pulled the club loose, though the old man resisted momentarily.

"A strange-looking club," said Shona, holding it to the light.

Falken studied the club. It seemed vaguely familiar. Pictures he had seen in the biosphere came to mind. Then, he recognized the old man's weapon.

Falken chuckled. "I'll be damned."

"You recognize this weapon?"

"It's not a weapon. It's a tool used to play a game."

"What game?"

"Golf! It's an old golf club. Used in a game that was played before the Cataclysm."

Shona had obviously never heard of such a game. "Was the game entertaining?"

Reno laughed again. "From what I know . . . it was only entertaining for a few. Frustrating for everyone else."

"Why would anyone play such a game?"

"Good question!"

Chapter
Twenty-eight

★★★★★★★

Neshu's moan rose from the center of the village. It was a wailing crescendo that seemed to push back the light, painting the faces of the dead. Standing inside the rings made by the treads of the tanks, she clutched herself, wrapping both arms around her body. She swayed as she moaned, then dropped to her knees.

Jean Peterson ran to her, clutching her in her arms, but the woman tore away and began throwing dirt on herself. Her voice seemed to turn into something inhuman as her head swung around and around, turning her long braids into whips that lashed at her neck and face.

Puhaly felt as though his skin was suddenly alive and crawling from his bones. "Jesus fucking Christ! She's come unwound."

Jean ran to Creighton. "Do something, dammit!"

Creighton turned and yelled, "Get the medic!"

Shona tried to settle Neshu, but her strength seemed to match his. Finally, when the medic arrived, it took Puhaly, Creighton, and Shona to subdue her until the injected sedative took effect.

Neshu finally fell into Shona's arms. He carried her to Reno's air-conditioned IFV, which sat in the center of a defensive perimeter formed by the other MBT's and IFV's.

Ibo sat on the ground, utterly dazed by everything he

was seeing: machines that moved without being seen or heard.; voices that travelled through the night like those of ghosts; clothes that seemed unimaginable; light that shot from the fingers of men as though they had captured the sun in their hands; skin on humans the color of the White Rhino painted on his cave.

Had he gone insane?

Creighton walked over and sat down by Ibo. He motioned to Falken. "Give me that thing."

Falken handed TC the golf club. TC looked at it in amazement. "It must be more than a century old."

"He must be more than a century old," Puhaly mumbled.

The medic returned with his aid kit. "She'll be out for hours."

TC nodded at Ibo. "Give him the works, doc. But be gentle. I don't want his heart giving out from fright before Shona can get some answers."

Creighton and Falken walked off toward the darkness beyond the ring of light.

"I don't know what's out there, Reno. That's disturbing. I want you to take a recon team and follow these bastards' tracks. Stay close but stay out of sight. No contact. Report back in two days."

Falken saluted and left. That's when he heard one of his officers call his name.

"Commo from the old man. Radio relay from the Iron Horse."

Creighton listened to Clayton's voice and responded affirmatively.

Jean Peterson walked to Creighton. "What was that about?"

"We've been ordered to the next valley and hold position. There's another element en route to hook up with our position."

"What kind of element?"

Creighton shrugged. "The C in C didn't speak specifically. He just said to wait . . . and the next time we speak we'll be in better communication link."

They walked off together, toward where a group of men were waiting.

The rest of the night was spent burying the dead.

★★★★★★★★★★★★★★

PART THREE
THE FOURTH
VALLEY

★★★★★★★

★★★★★★★★★★★★★

Chapter
Twenty-nine

★★★★★★★

1000.

Ibo had seen strange sights in the past few hours; sights never before imagined. The tanks reminded him of the White Rhino in shape; the skin of the drivers in the color. But what he was looking at now shook him to the core of his being. He had never seen such a vision—and it had to be a vision—for there was nothing on earth that could do what he saw coming in his direction.

A huge bird approached. Rather, a bat, like the bats who shared his cave. But this bat was tremendous in size, and he knew it must be ferocious. Like in the cave, he would play the game with his club and a stone to kill the bat, though he doubted this particular bat would be as easily destroyed as the bats in the cave.

The game was simple: throwing a rock in the air lured the bat, which thought the rock was an insect. When the bat neared the stone, and with the right timing, Ibo would swing as the bat neared the range of the club.

He picked up a rock and threw it into the air, watching it fall to earth, knowing the bat would chase the stone and fly into the path of his swinging club. Ibo's old arm arced toward the sky; the stone flew from his ancient fingers, soaring into the sky, though not as high as in his youth. He perched the club on his shoulder, prepared to strike the large bat as it chased the stone into his killing zone.

The stone reached its zenith, then fell, thudding on the ground beside Ibo.

The great bat remained in the sky, though lower, but not low enough to strike.

A roar of astonishment went up from the soldiers. The men scrambled from the tanks and vehicles in the mouth of his valley and formed a group. All eyes stared at the bat, which was banking, flying lower, on a straight line for the open area outside the circle formed by the vehicles.

"I'll be damned," said Creighton.

"I've heard of this . . . but I thought it was bullshit," said Puhaly.

The giant bat-shaped wing came closer to the ground, its engines humming as the landing gear extended. There was a wisp of dust from the wing-tip vortices as the aircraft made contact with the earth.

As the energy of forward momentum played out, the aircraft slowed to a stop in front of the bivouac area. The canopy opened; the pilot stood and removed a helmet. Captain Alissa Breen shook her head, allowing her long hair to fall to her shoulders.

Thunder One had been deployed to the forward edge of the battle area.

Chapter Thirty

★★★★★★★

Creighton and Breen were standing beside Thunder One. The rest of the troops circled the aircraft, still not quite certain of what they were seeing. This was the first time any of them had heard of the flying machine.

"What's your mission, captain?" asked Creighton.

"I'm part of an advanced element, Captain Creighton," the pilot explained. "There are several teams of scientists that are to begin establishing a communications network from Base Camp One to the farthest controlled area. The network is called GroundStar. It's part of the Dawson Belt, named after President Dawson. It will provide world-wide communications."

"What is your part in the GroundStar project?"

"My mission is in two parts. First, by flying air recon-naissance I can examine likely sites for installations. Second, to provide security. Thunder One is a tank killer. I'm not armed at present. Colonel Clayton wants me to fly pure reconnaissance at the present."

Creighton thought he detected a note of dissatisfac-tion in her voice as he turned and studied the aircraft. It was a fascinating piece of machinery, and one that could be invaluable.

Captain Breen ran her hand along the leading edge of the wing, checking for any damage that might have been caused during landing.

"What exactly is this Dawson Belt?"

She bent down and drew a rough outline in the dirt. It was shaped like the continent.

"A string of microwave transmitting stations that will link our forces in a single commo net. At present you're using relays from unit to unit to reach the command center. GroundStar will provide direct communications to command. As the campaign moves farther south, communications will be more difficult to maintain. GroundStar will be able to communicate with each individual unit in the field."

Creighton looked toward the mountains surrounding the valley. "I suppose this area will be the site of a station."

She nodded. "Colonel Clayton thought the presence of the reserve and a GroundStar base would complement each other."

"When will the station be installed?" Dr. Jean Peterson joined the conversation.

"The project—your reserve and GroundStar—are to be conducted concurrently. The GroundStar equipment will be transported with the animals from end of track as soon as the area is secure."

Creighton climbed up the ladder into the cockpit. The instrument panel was vaguely familiar; some of the instrumentation was similar to the console of his MBT.

"Is there room for two?"

She smiled. "It'll be a tight fit, but it can be done. There's an observer seat behind the primary seat. Uncomfortable . . . but adequate."

Creighton looked to the south, in the direction the Marauder tanks were moving.

"How would you feel about going to work, captain?"

"What do you need?"

Creighton explained. "There's an enemy element operating in this area. I want to know their exact location. Would you perform an airborne recon?"

"That shouldn't be a problem. However, I'm under strict orders not to engage the enemy."

"A reconnaissance flight, captain. Nothing more.

How soon can you be ready to fly?"

"Ten minutes."

"Good," Creighton said. "There's just one more thing."

"What might that be? As if I don't already know."

Creighton grinned. "You're going to have a passenger."

★★★★★★★★★★★★★

Chapter
Thirty-one

★★★★★★★★

The view from 2,000 feet was more breathtaking than Creighton had imagined. What he could see to the north was mostly beige in color; to the south and east, foliage turned the earth green. It was a beautiful contrast, especially when he looked west and saw the blue of the Atlantic ocean.

Breen was sitting in front of him; he was cramped in an auxiliary jump seat situated behind her main seat. Strapped in with a harness, Creighton had a clear view over her head. There was no noticeable noise, only the dull roar of the jet engine.

Unlike jets of the twenty-first century, Thunder One was not outfitted with the sophisticated equipment that provided counter measures for air combat or ground-based missile attacks. Thunder One was in a class by itself; the only operational aircraft on earth, therefore, the systems aboard were limited to flight, navigation, and limited armament composed primarily of ground-target acquisition lasers. The weapons platforms had AGM, air-to-ground laser-guided missiles, and cannon.

"It's similar to your main battle tank, captain. You have basically three elements: a machine, weapons platforms, and personnel. A fighting aircraft has the same components. The main difference is that Thunder One can go into the air, and move a little faster."

"How fast?"

She shook her head. "Not Mach speed, like in the old days. Two hundred knots is the edge of the envelope. But that's more than enough. The air combat threat doesn't exist per se, therefore speed and turn rate aren't essential. What's essential is weight. The limited surface area dictates the amount of solar energy that can be produced, which establishes the weight limitations."

"What about maneuverability?"

Rather than answer, she executed an aileron roll, turning the aircraft upside down.

Creighton felt his weight sag against the restraint of the harness. A momentary feeling of fear was quickly suppressed as he realized he was secure.

"What now?"

"We'll split the *S*"

Thunder One dove upside down toward earth with Breen pulling back on the yoke. Creighton saw the horizon begin to appear; then the aircraft was level, flying in the opposite direction.

Creighton laughed. "Fantastic! All right. I'm convinced. Now, let's get to work." He pointed in the direction he suspected the Marauder tank unit was moving.

Thunder One eased onto course.

Ten minutes later, flying at 3,000 feet, the tank tracks of the Marauder unit appeared as lines drawn through the lush landscape.

The tracks led east, then south, where the jungle ended abruptly against a mountain range.

"They're in the mountains," Creighton said.

Breen eased back on the yoke, then banked toward the mountain range. At 10,000 feet, they were level with a ridge running along the tops of the mountains.

"Let's find out what's on the other side, captain." Creighton motioned with his hand for the pilot to go over the mountain range.

A series of long valleys appeared, spreading eastward like fingers extending from the palm of a hand. The topography was mostly rolling hills that appeared to laze at the foot of the higher range. Trees rose in greater abundance than Creighton had seen anywhere on earth.

"Breathtakingly beautiful," said Breen. She had never seen such a sight either.

Turbulence shook the aircraft slightly as she pushed the nose forward. Creighton only heard a whisper as the wing-shaped aircraft began a descent into the valley.

Then he saw something that he recognized, and felt his stomach tighten.

"Christ! Get out of here!"

The green carpet below suddenly appeared sprinkled with golden sparks followed by puffs of smoke.

"Settle down, captain. We're safe," Breen said. "Their artillery isn't designed for aircraft."

"The hell you say. They've got machine guns!" He pointed to the jungle where tracer fire rode up like a stream of fire.

"Get the hell out of here."

Breen shoved the power throttle forward and was pulling back on the yoke when there was a shudder. The whisper of the engine fell quiet. Creighton felt Thunder One begin to sink. Breen pulled off her helmet and looked over her shoulder. "Hold on. We're going down."

Creighton reached past her to the microphone on the instrument console. "Lion squadron leader to Fireball."

Falken's voice came over the receiver.

Creighton spoke quickly, but calmly. "Reno . . . we've been hit by ground elements. We're going down." He could see that the nose of Thunder One was aimed at one of the valleys shaped like on index finger. "There's a mountain range approximately forty miles from your location. Beyond the mountain range—to the east— there's a series of valleys extending eastward. We're going into the fourth valley."

Creighton carefully detailed the course Falken was to follow in order to reach the valley. When finished, he added, "Contact the C in C. Tell him we'll destroy the aircraft before we'll let it be captured."

That was when the mountain range blocked off further communication. Thunder One settled into an approach toward what appeared to be a long stretch of open flat terrain.

"An old dried-out riverbed." Breen was pointing at the only spot where she could land.

Easing onto the heading, Creighton felt the slight thump of the landing gear extending and locking into place. The wheels touched down the aircraft lurched, then settled into a bumpy roll. Thirty seconds later, it came to a halt.

Creighton stood up as the canopy opened. Only one thought came to mind.

"Shit!"

★★★★★★★★★★★★★
Chapter Thirty-two
★★★★★★★

"Move! Find them!" Major Vita Slazenger ordered her men. She didn't know what had appeared over their bivouac, but her training told her it must be two things: the enemy, and important. She could score a major coup if the machine were recovered. After all, the secrets of flight was something their technicians had not recovered from the previous inhabitants of the biospheres.

By some quirk, all the information regarding flight had been erased from the computers, and all pictures and books containing information had disappeared. It was as though flight were some form of previous evil the people of the past had feared. Yet the Marauder society had heard stories of flying machines, but no one believed that they were true. Tanks were heavy; too heavy to fly.

How could a machine get off the ground and fly into combat?

Slazenger had thought it impossible. Until now. Which spurred her toward the direction the airplane had been descending.

The tanks moved into column formation, and Slazenger gave the order. "Flank speed." Then she slipped into the commander's chair and closed the cupola.

"I'll find the flying machine and bring it to headquarters as a prize," she said aloud.

She released a throaty laugh as she sped away, thinking only one thought: The driver of the machine must be kept alive until Slazenger was given the secret of flight.

Then she could name her price, and her place, in the Marauder army!

* * * * * * *

Chapter
Thirty-three

★★★★★★★★

1300.

"Damn!" Clayton slammed down the telephone in his office at headquarters. He turned to Dr. Paul Shoemaker. Short, trim, with a balding head and drooping mustache, Shoemaker had the habit of pulling at it when worried. Clayton watched the man nearly tear the cultivated brush of hair from the top of his lip.

"Disastrous. And such a fine young woman," Shoemaker mumbled. He walked to the window and looked outside. The building's long shadow stretched toward three lorries carrying the equipment that would compose the first GroundStar station on the continent. GS-1, its designation, was being unloaded. In a long line of lorries sat more equipment that would be transported to the south for the building of other installations in the communications link that would follow the advance of the military push.

Clayton stared hard into the scientist's face. "Damn you, Shoemaker. You sound like all is lost. That she and my tank commander are both dead."

Shoemaker shrugged, then pointed out the value of the airplane to his project as he glanced again through the window.

"We were going to rely on the aircraft for forward observation to locate new sites for the GroundStar. It would appear we've now lost that option. Our project will be slowed down if we have to wait for ground forces to survey the higher elevations."

Clayton was at the point of becoming angry, but suppressed the desire to twist off the scientist's pointed nose.

"You give up too easily, professor. My forces have reported Thunder One went down in an area some distance from the enemy unit operating in that area. Which, I might add, is a greater concern than your precious GroundStar."

Shoemaker looked surprised. "Why is that of greater importance than communications?"

Clayton explained in a voice that was calm. "We already have communications. Not as sophisticated as GroundStar, but workable. What we don't need is for Thunder One to fall into the hands of the Marauders. We know they don't have flight capability. But they might . . . if they recover Thunder One. These bastards are very resourceful at duplicating. We've had the edge in this war due to our technology. A weapon like Thunder One could swing the balance to their side. They could push this force off the continent. That's of greater concern than a communications center."

What Clayton withheld, but was thinking, was that in addition to the loss of the aircraft there was another dread. One of a more personal nature.

He considered Captain Creighton as he would a son. Removing a picture from his jacket pocket, he studied the faces of a young woman holding a small boy. Abraham Creighton and his mother. The only woman Colonel Thomas Clayton had ever loved. She had married Clayton's childhood friend, and she was later killed in the desert.

There was a knock on the door. Roman Standish entered. Poet, philosopher, mathematician, astronomer, historian—man for all seasons and teacher to TC Creighton and other members of AfriKorps who grew up in the Vegas Biosphere.

Which was why he now looked concerned. "Is it true about Captain Creighton?" asked Roman.

Clayton looked at him in utter amazement. "How in the hell did you know?" He automatically looked at the telephone. "I just received the information myself."

Roman's right eyebrow arched. "Many of your officers were students of mine, sir."

Clayton grumped, "One of them wouldn't be a signal officer who relayed the transmission from the commo center?"

Roman's face flashed a cherubic smile.

Clayton waved off the response, then sat at his desk. Roman walked over and lightly touched Clayton's folded hands.

"He'll be all right. You trained him. Remember?"

Clayton nodded, then cleared his throat. He glanced at Shoemaker. "Everything that can be done for the aircraft and personnel is being done. Falken's en route with a combat patrol of MBT's and IFV's. If they're alive, they'll be found. Right now we have another matter to consider."

Shoemaker spoke up. "Installing GroundStar."

Roman looked confused. "What is GroundStar?"

After Shoemaker explained, Clayton reached across his desk and turned on a device that flashed a hologram into the thin air. The hologram was a map of the African continent. Red stars were located at certain points from one end of the continent to the other.

"Each of the red stars is placed at the approximate point Dr. Shoemaker feels will be needed to establish the relay stations for GroundStar. The site designated GS-4 will be in the area where the zoologists are establishing the game reserve. Shoemaker is preparing to load his equipment onto the Iron Horse and go downrange to end of track. He'll pick up a military escort—Captain Armbrust—and proceed to the location selected for GS-4."

"That's near the location the airplane went down," Roman noted.

"They went down approximately forty miles to the southeast."

"Shona is with that expedition, is that correct?"

"That's correct. Along with the zoology personnel."

After a pause, Roman requested, "May I accompany Dr. Shoemaker?"

"What for? I thought you hated the heat."

"I do. It's dreadful. But I'm bored. Shona is the only man I can talk with. Besides . . . I would like to see the game reserve." His face became clouded. "Recalling that request you made . . . If captain Creighton is alive, what I need to tell him should be said at some distance from your location. Don't you agree?"

Colonel Clayton clasped his hands behind his back and stared at the toes of his boots. "Perhaps you're right."

Roman spoke again. "I understand the animals are with Captain Armbrust."

"You understand correctly. Armbrust will provide security for the transportation of the animals and the GroundStar personnel. The area is now secure and the next phase of the project can begin."

Shoemaker interrupted with a question that was bothering him. "Why the rush on the animals? I should think GroundStar is more important."

Clayton smiled. "To you, perhaps. Not to the animals. They're getting close to mating time."

Chapter
Thirty-four

★★★★★★★★

Creighton's sweat-drenched face peered over Captain Alissa Breen's shoulder; her body was bent over the engine cowling, which was open, exposing the aircraft's damaged power plant.

"It could be worse. A piece of shrapnel punctured one of the solar leads connected to the turbine."

Creighton understood. The MBT's ran off the same principle: solar power produced by the outer solar skin fed to batteries which supplied electrical power to the power plant.

"Can you make repairs?"

She nodded. "Yes. But not here. I'll need a new lead cable. I'm afraid—unlike your tanks—airplanes don't carry spare parts."

Creighton looked up at the sun, setting near the ridgeline of the mountain range. "It'll be dark soon. We're going to have to secure the aircraft, then start walking toward our forces."

She shook her head. "You go. I'll stay with the airplane."

Creighton grabbed her by the arm and turned her around, facing him. "You'll do as I say, captain. You've been assigned to my command. That means you'll follow my orders. My orders are to conceal the aircraft and start infiltrating toward our forces."

She pulled away. "A pilot is the commander of an aircraft, captain. I'm staying."

"You don't have an aircraft, captain. You have what amounts to a decommissioned piece of junk. You're going. That's final." TC touched the butt of the pistol strapped to his hip.

She noticed the seriousness in his voice, and with that, something peculiar—she sensed he was afraid. Not for himself. But for her.

"I've seen what they do to prisoners," TC hissed.

She swallowed hard, then nodded. "Whatever you say, captain."

"Come on. Let's get this aircraft under cover."

With great effort, the two soldiers pushed Thunder One from the dried riverbed to the thick jungle nearby. For the next hour the two cut branches to conceal the aircraft; a large branch was used to wipe out the tracks left in the soft dirt.

That was when they heard the groan of approaching armor. A plume of dark exhaust smoke rose in the distance, mixing with the dust of the advancing column.

"Let's get out of here," Creighton ordered.

Breen was carrying the survival kit from the aircraft that included two days' water, food, and an automatic rifle. Before she left Thunder One she completed her last obligation to the aircraft as pilot-in-command. She armed the tamper-proof self-destruct mechanism that would detonate if the canopy were opened.

"Let's go!" TC ordered.

The two Americans crossed the riverbed, wiping their tracks as they moved backward. As the column rounded the river bend leading to the makeshift runway, Creighton and Breen lay concealed in the treeline overlooking the riverbed.

Creighton held his binoculars to his eyes and studied the lead tank. A red pennant attached to a radio antenna signalled to Creighton he was watching the commander's tank. He saw the cupola open and a blonde woman appear.

Slazenger dismounted and walked along the

riverbed. She paused occasionally, squatted and studied the ground, then looked toward the two opposing tree-lines bordering the river.

Creighton noted she had a hunter's gait; she was obviously skilled as a tracker. Not animals, since there were hardly any left in Africa.

People.

She seemed to be adept at tracking people, and had he known her better, he would have realized he couldn't have been more accurate.

As a child she was taught by her father to track people. To look for the telltale spoor of the human prey. A rock overturned, a scruff in the dirt, left by the running, stumbling quarry that had been reduced to raw, running meat.

Carefully, she scoured the riverbed.

"Damn! She knows her stuff," Creighton breathed.

He saw the Marauder kneel by the spot where Thunder One had come to rest after the landing.

Slazenger's hand disappeared into the rocky terrain. Through the field glasses, Creighton saw her put something to her nose.

"What has she found?" Breen asked.

Creighton shook his head. "I don't know."

Major Vita Slazenger held a shredded leaf to her nose. It had been torn, as though rubbed harshly against another object. She bent over and smelled the dirt, and the rocks lying on the surface.

Chlorophyll!

In the next instant she was on her feet barking orders to the gunner who was standing behind a machine gun on her tank. From the rear of the column a lorry appeared; nearly two dozen troops dismounted and began following the direction of her pointing arm, toward where Thunder One lay camouflaged.

"Let's get out of here," Creighton whispered.

Breen pulled away from his grip. "No. I have to know what happens to the aircraft."

He tried to reason with her. "You armed the self-destruct mechanism. If they pop the canopy the demolition will take care of the aircraft."

She shook her head. "I've got to know!"

She took the binoculars and stared at Slazenger, who was strutting over the riverbed toward the opposite bank. Rage coursed through her body as she sensed the inevitable. How she hated the swaggering bitch who was walking directly toward the piece of machinery that Breen herself had helped design, and had been entrusted with to bring to the other side of the world.

The hate heightened as she heard the loud voices of Slazenger's soldiers from the treeline.

Slazenger broke into a run toward the soldiers, and Captain Breen knew all hope was lost.

"You're right," she said softly. "Let's go. I only hope that bitch is the one who opens the canopy. When we hear the explosion . . . I'll have that much satisfaction."

They both turned and eased their way toward the direction Creighton knew Falken would have to travel in order to find the fourth valley.

An hour later, the two Americans had not heard the detonation of the self-destruct mechanism.

Chapter
Thirty-five

★★★★★★★

1900.

Creighton was sitting against a large boulder; looking up, he could barely see through the thick canopy of branches blocking the sky. It was dusk, but nearly black in the valley where the sun had long since slid behind the mountain range.

Alissa was sitting beside him, sipping from a canteen. Her hair was tangled; her face coated with a mixture of sweat and dust from the evasive march away from Thunder One. He could see the lost look in her eyes; the same look he had had the day he buried Silver.

"Airplanes can be replaced. People can't," he reminded her in a soothing voice.

She shifted, rubbing her arms; the skin was scratched. He remembered observing that before it had grown dark. Reaching to her, he took her arm and poured water over the scratches. He felt her wince and pull slightly, then relax.

Creighton realized it was the first time he had touched a woman since he last touched his wife.

"Sorry." His voice drifted up into the night, carrying a note of sadness that fell heavily back to Alissa.

"There's something that you should know, Abraham."

Creighton sat up. He couldn't recall the last time he had been called Abraham, except by his wife. She had always called him Abraham, or Abe. To everyone else he

114

was TC, or Creighton.

"What's that?" There was genuine curiousity in his voice.

"Silver and I were friends. We knew each other as children in the Vegas Biosphere. I knew you as well . . . you just don't remember me. I remember all of you. Reno. Roman. When my father was transferred to Biosphere One to join the General Staff, it was the worst day of my life."

"'Skinny Lissie," Creighton blurted. "I'll be damned. I remember you. You were always tagging along with me, Reno, and Silver."

She nodded, but wasn't offended by the nickname. "I'm not skinny any longer."

He looked approvingly at her. "You certainly aren't. You've filled out wonderfully. I wish Silver could see you." He stopped abruptly. It was as though the words were lost to him.

"Colonel Clayton gave me a briefing before I left Base Camp One. About her death. I learned about it six months ago. He filled in the details."

Creighton said nothing. Finally, he said, "Did he tell you I hold him responsible?"

"Yes. He said you might not speak kindly of him."

"Kindly? I respect the man as a soldier. I despise him as a man."

"In that case . . . you will understand how I feel about you."

Creighton sat up suddenly. "What the hell do you mean?"

"You'll understand that I hold you responsible for the loss of my aircraft. Like you hold Colonel Clayton responsible for the loss of your wife. It's the same type of situation. If he hadn't had orders cut for her to come to Africa she might still be alive. If you hadn't had me fly you over this area my airplane would be safe. So would I. I guess if I die . . . you'll be to blame for that as well. That is, if your logic is accurate. . . . and you're a fair person."

"That's bullshit."

"That's truth. I'm merely applying your reasoning in a personal situation to my present situation. You should understand that, captain."

Creighton wrapped his arms around himself. "Airplanes and people are two different things, captain."

"Perhaps. But what may be important to one person may have less importance to another. And vice versa. Like the old saying, 'one man's junk is another man's treasure.'"

"I find people more important than airplanes."

"So do I. Which is why I don't blame you. But I could . . . if I wanted to be unforgiving. To hold a grudge."

Creighton fumbled through the survival kit and opened a packet of dehydrated soybean soup and poured water into it. The packet was lined with a special chemical that became hot once mixed with water, rising to the temperature of 225 degrees fahrenheit. After remaining intact for an hour, the packet's biodegradable material would begin dissolving.

Spooning a mouthful of the soup, he thought about what she had said.

"It's hard to stop loving someone, Alissa. Someone you have known all your life and dreamed of living with until old age. I miss her. I miss the children we will never have. The life we'll never have." He could see a star shine through a tiny opening in the canopy overhead. "I miss her presence."

Her hand touched his forearm and gently squeezed, a human gesture not lost to the Cataclysm.

"I know," she whispered. Then she stood and took the compass she carried in the pocket of her flight suit. "It's life's longing for itself. It's called love."

She extended her hand to him in the darkness and he seemed to sense the offering. He took her hand and felt her stength as she pulled him to his feet.

"Come on," she said. "Let's keep moving."

Chapter Thirty-six

★★★★★★★

2200.

Roman Standish stood awestruck at what he perceived to be one of the most important moments in the history of Africa since the Cataclysm. But Captain Armbrust wasn't as impressed.

"They smell like death warmed over, Roman. I haven't smelled anything like it in my lifetime."

The aroma of the animals filled the air where the holding pens had been erected near the end of track. The smell of fresh manure was something unique to the soldiers of AfriKorps. But not to Roman, who used to visit the stock biomes frequently at the Vegas Biosphere. He rather enjoyed the smell. It was invigorating, reminding him of an earlier time.

Slaughter animals were not to be returned to the environment, though some species had been retained for research purposes. The methane, and need to destroy the forests to provide grazing land, had been a contributing factor to the greenhouse effect.

But the cultured preservation of earth's wildlife had been considered important. The wise men and women plotting the future knew that if earth was to recover, it had to do so with natural—as well as human—contribution. But only at a certain pace.

"When are we leaving?" asked Roman.

"Sunrise. The animals will be crated and loaded onto

lorries. TC and his unit have cleared the area to the valley."

"You know about TC?"

Armbrust nodded. He absent-mindedly pulled at the black patch over his right eye, remembering it was Creighton who rescued him from the Marauders. "I know. There's been no word."

"He'll be safe."

Armbrust tried to steer away from the conversation. "What about the GroundStar technicians?"

"They'll accompany the animals. It'll be like a combination of Noah's Ark and the Pied Piper."

Both men laughed, but the laughter was cut short by the shout of a soldier from near the train. In the distance, beyond the camp, one of the scout motorcycles hummed toward the south.

Armbrust, followed by Roman, hurried to where a young soldier was kneeling by another. Roman stood there as Armbrust checked the body. He rolled the soldier over, then turned away.

Roman gasped as the soldier's face shone with the mask of death beneath the light of the moon.

"My God," said Roman. "How could he have gotten here?"

Armbrust looked at the train. Then he recalled the dozen or more attendants recruited from the pacified hostile tribes to tend the animals.

"He must have slipped aboard the train, then avoided everyone until nightfall."

Roman turned and shook his fist at the south. Beneath him, on the ground, the young soldier's face provided the most damning evidence of his murderer's identity.

The soldier's eyes were missing. Two empty, bloody orbs absorbed the moonlight where only minutes before the light of youth and life had danced.

Both men recognized the mark of Benhaddou!

Chapter Thirty-seven

★★★★★★★

Slazenger sat in the flicker of firelight, watching the faces of the younger officers assigned to her patrol. With all her strength she had suppressed the overall glee she was feeling at having discovered the American flying machine. She withheld the urge to gloat; to point out that it was she who had suspected the airplane might be booby-trapped. It was what she would have done to prevent the enemy from having a secret.

She took a stick and drew a line in the dirt. "We will leave in the morning and travel south, then west to the coast. General Burril's headquarters are not scheduled to withdraw to the south for three days. We will report . . . and give him the flying machine. He will know what to do with the machine."

Rolf Vandergon, a muscular, blond officer who had often made advances to Slazenger asked the obvious. "What about the driver? Why is the machine important if it can't be flown?"

She shook her head. Her army was being systematically pushed south by the advancing AfriKorps and all because of technology. The technology had to be captured and copied before it could be mastered.

"We can learn to fly the machine. In time. It will be difficult. But it's not impossible. For the first time since AfriKorps arrived we have a valuable piece of their technology that can advance our tactics and weaponry."

Vandergon seemed to understand. As he understood the darting of Slazenger's eyes toward her tent as she rose. The other officers went back to their tanks. Vandergon went to the tent. He walked inside to find Slazenger standing nude before her cot.

She had a glow in her eyes he had never seen in a woman before. He felt himself harden, and before he could loosen his trousers she was on him, her arm moving with the speed of lightning. There was a sharp tear; then another. In the light within the tent he saw the burnished glow of a sharp knife. Looking down, he saw that he was practically naked from the waist down. The knife slashes had stripped him of his trousers.

Her breath was hot in his ear; her breasts pushed hard against his chest, and she took his member with such ferocity that he thought he would scream.

But the only scream was from her, when she climaxed on top of his chest. And he thought of how she made him feel impotent as a soldier. As an officer.

But in this joining of the flesh he was revitalized by her screams. In the jungle, surrounded by threat, his mind began to contrive other, more sinister thoughts.

Thrusting into her, watching her eyes glaze, he told himself how easily the airplane could be his.

He teased her with his performance, which she thought was the best she had ever enjoyed. His only mistake was in obviously enjoying her writhing and weakness during her orgasms, when she was the most vulnerable. When she couldn't command him, nor herself. His pride shone through and she felt the treachery as though his fleshy spear communicated it to her wet receptacle and transmitted the treacherous message to her brain.

That was when her arm flashed again, the knife rising and falling, like her body during her final orgasm. During his final orgasm. His final moment of life.

The prize was hers! She would share it with no man!

0600.

Creighton felt their presence before he smelled the foul odor of their bodies drifting on the slight breeze flowing under the jungle canopy. He tensed, then relaxed; the soldier's instincts took command as he closed his hand around Alissa's mouth. He felt her body stiffen as she awoke in fright. When she realized who was holding her she relaxed and listened to his whisper.

"We have intruders. I count ten. We're surrounded. Two are in the trees. Take your pistol and move back to back. We have to make a stand."

He could feel that she wanted to speak, but she resisted and obeyed, moving around to his back until she felt their spines touch.

Again he whispered over his shoulder while glancing around.

"When I fire . . . they'll attack. Kill anything that you see. Maintain fire in your section. Don't worry about mine. I'll take care of your back. You take care of mine. Ready?"

He felt her nod as she slipped her automatic pistol from her holster, remembering the magazine held thirty-four armor piercing needlelike flachettes that had the penetrating and destructive power of a .45-caliber projectile.

The flachettes were composed of a special alloy.

121

When fired, the gas of the gun powder turned them into round bullets. This allowed for more rounds to be carried in a smaller magazine, turning a pistol into a small, light machine gun.

Creighton raised the automatic rifle he had recovered from Thunder One. Looking up, he could see the slight movement of a branch over his head; another branch moved near the trunk of a low-hanging tree under which they were sitting.

To run would be senseless. He knew from experience, when armed with superior weaponry, the way to deal with a hostile ambush was to let them attack into the withering firepower they carried.

From nearby rocks he saw a head appear. A dark-haired figure was framed against the thin light beginning to filter through the overhead canopy.

Creighton's finger flicked off the safety. He took a deep breath and didn't say a word. His weapon was all he needed to start the fray.

A long tongue of tracer fire exploded from the muzzle, tearing directly into the branches overhead. The suddenness with which it began caught the intruders off-guard, as Creighton had hoped.

The second intruder in the trees stared unbelievingly at the man beside him, who twitched and jerked in the branches, finally dropping his spear as his body pitched forward.

That was when Creighton fired again, striking the second intruder flush in the chest and casually waltzing the line of fire up the chest to the head. The intruder's brains left his skull before his feet left the branch.

That was when all hell broke loose beneath the canopy.

"Fire at dead center!" Creighton shouted.

Alissa saw the first hostile enter her field of fire from over a large boulder. She fired as his arm arched toward her. A spear flew wildly past her shoulder, nearly striking Creighton in the back of the head.

The hostile dropped to his knees and crawled at her, clutching the entrails oozing from a gaping hole in his stomach. She wanted to feel pity. She fired again instead. The man quit crawling a few feet from where she fired again at another man coming at her from another angle.

A curious thought invaded her mind; a simply ridiculous thought: *They're so small! Like children Am I killing children?*

The horror of the thought evaporated as her finger closed sharply around the trigger. The weapon jumped twice; the hostile pitched backward, lying with his head touching his ass, his arms splayed out as though praying to the heavens.

Creighton took out three more with methodical accuracy. One to the left. One in the middle. One to the right. Smoke wafted from his rifle's barrel. Through the cloud he saw the eerie image of another appear. He fired as Alissa fired again. Their spines touched, driven together by the recoil of their discharging weapons.

The last hostile released a long, howling shriek, charging as he threw his spear. Alissa fired. The man kept charging.

Creighton wondered why she wasn't firing. He rolled away and unleashed a deadly volume of automatic fire. The noise rose up to the trees, then splattered back to the ground, turning the enclosed area into a din.

The hostile spun as the striking bullets turned him like a dancer pirhouetting on stage. As he turned and swirled, blood flew from the rents where the bullets had turned flesh to shredded pulp. The man fell face forward, landing in Alissa's lap.

"God!" She screamed. "O-o-o-h-h-h! Get him off! Get him off." Her voice was nearly hysterical.

That was when Creighton realized why she couldn't remove the dead man from her body. Not because she wasn't strong enough. Or the fact that there wasn't enough leverage. She was pinned to the earth with a sharp spear driven through her leg and into the ground.

Creighton threw off the dead body. The smell of cordite stung his nostrils; the copperish taste of fear and adrenalin burned in his mouth.

"Sit still," he ordered. Examining the spear's entry, he could see the shaft had driven through the fleshy part of her right thigh.

"It could be worse. It missed the femoral artery."

She didn't seem to find any immediate solace in the observation.

"I can't move," she said with a voice tinged slightly by fear and pain.

"You don't have to. Just sit tight. I'll take care of you."

Creighton removed a small tourniquet from the first-aid kit taken from Thunder One. He looped the restraining device around her leg just above where the spear had penetrated.

Without explanation, he looked up and said, "I'll be damned—look up there, in the tree. The beautiful bird."

The moment her head came up, her eyes on the tree, her chin exposed perfectly, Creighton's right fist slammed into the point of her chin. Her head sagged as she thundered into unconsciousness.

Moving quickly, Creighton tightened the tourniquet with all his strength; when the blood flow was stanched, he gripped the shaft of the spear and gave a sharp jerk.

The spear came out, leaving a slimy red trail across her boots.

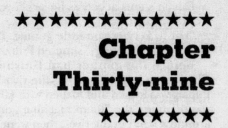

★★★★★★★★★★★★★

Chapter
Thirty-nine

★★★★★★★★

0900.

Reno Falken heard Puhaly cursing from the opened hatch of Ribald's Chariot. Falken was riding in the tank commander's chair, preferring to command TC's tank rather than his customary IFV. There was a simple philosophy to this act: when he found TC, he wanted his old friend to see his MBT had come to the rescue.

Puhaly had been the driving force throughout the night search for first the entry to the fourth valley, then the trail left by the two downed soldiers. The gunner had been so overcome by anger and frustration from losing Creighton that he was like a raging bull. It was the only time Falken had ever known Fergus not to chide and rib the gunner.

All knew they had to keep quiet and stay serious now. Puhaly would eat blood-raw any man in the search team that threatened recovery of Creighton. He was pacified only when they found the tracks leading away from where the Marauder patrol had recovered Thunder One.

It was at that point that Reno made one of the most difficult decisions of his life: duty over friendship. Rather than have the entire element committed to finding their comrades, he sent the remainder of the rescue force onto the trail of the Marauders.

Puhaly suddenly shouted. He pointed to the sky. "Look! In the sky!"

Falken's guts ached as he saw three vultures flying in a circular pattern.

"Hit it, Fergus, you little gnome. Drive like there was a hot woman waiting!" shouted Puhaly.

Before the gunner had finished the words, the Chariot was streaking along the riverbed at flank speed. Puhaly was locked and loaded with HEAT rounds. Falken was manning the 30mm machine gun. The MBT roared around a bend in the river, then went cross-country.

"Obstacle to the front!" shouted Falken.

Puhaly peered through his GPS, gunner primary sight, and pressed the laser rangefinder switch. The massive boulder's range was lased-fed back and Puhaly fired.

The 120mm cannon roared with the report of the high-explosive shell leaving the barrel. It expectorated a thin wisp of smoke, then there was the explosion. The boulder disappeared from the path. The Chariot rode over the rubble unimpeded.

Eighty meters later, they rolled to a halt beneath the jungle canopy. The sight greeting them nearly made their stomachs turn. Black bodies were being shredded by black vultures.

"Jesus," said Puhaly. "But at least we know who's having who for breakfast."

One body squirmed at the midsection where a vulture had poked his head into a bullet hole and was eating the entrails from the inside of the stomach cavity.

Puhaly opened up with a volume of machine gun fire from the 7.62 co-axial. The birds stormed into the air, screeching and flapping their wings. Puhaly climbed out and examined the bodies.

"Hostiles. Damned strange-looking critters. They look like they might be related to Fergus."

The dead bodies were different in size than anything Falken had ever seen. They had the appearance of grown men—the size and shape of children.

"Pigmies," said Falken. "They must be descendants of

Pigmies. They were a midgetlike people who lived to the west before the Cataclysm."

"I know what the bloody buggers were. Fuck the anthropology lesson!" snapped Puhaly. "Where is TC!"

Falken looked around. Then he found what he thought was his answer. "There! In the dirt. There's tracks."

Puhaly found the two tracks etched into the dirt in a long continuous trail. Thin and narrow. He looked around. He could see where branches had been cut from the trees. Shredded leaves and twigs lay on the ground near a small pool of what appeared to be blood.

"Saddle up!" ordered Falken.

Puhaly climbed aboard and the Chariot stormed away, hot on the trail of the tracks leading north to the next valley.

★★★★★★★★★★★★★
Chapter
Forty
★★★★★★★

Creighton leaned into the straps from his and Alissa's belt used to form a harness on the travois he had fashioned from branches cut from the tree. She was still unconscious, lying on crossties he had secured to the two main support poles with the laces from her boots and strips of cloth from his jacket. The harness cut into his muscles, but he never stopped.

He kept marching. Left. Right. Left. Right.

March or die! His brain ordered his body. And his body obeyed.

Where was it? he asked himself. When was it like this moment? Then he remembered.

In DESFOR. He and Puhaly had been sent into the desert on foot. They both had been recruits. They both had been younger, more easily frightened. But not after that baptism of Hell.

The Christening it was called.

The Christening was required of every soldier. Three days in the desert without food or water. Three days among hostiles, forced to survive; to prove their worthiness before being given equipment worth more than life itself if captured by the hostiles.

Both men worked together, one on guard during the day while the other slept; avoiding marching through the heat. Marching at night, their eyes and other senses alert to the danger that existed.

In the end, Puhaly twisted his ankle and Creighton had to carry his old friend.

Both reached the reception station together. As it had to be. Both men had to return, or neither returned at all. Even if it meant one carried the dead body of his comrade.

It was the tradition of the old way. The toughest survived. The weaker stayed in the biomes. The desert was for only the bold and courageous.

He tightened his grip on the harness, lifting the straps slightly to allow a fresh flow of blood into his arms where the straps had cut off the flow.

Looking up, he saw the sun. They were out from under the canopy and onto a plain at the base of the valley. On the other side was the third valley. He pushed on, but was stopped a moan from Alissa.

Setting down the travois, he opened the tourniquet, allowing the blood to flow to her lower leg as he had every hour since he had begun the march out.

She was delirious and he suspected the little hostiles had dipped their spears into some kind of poison.

Bastards!

That was when he heard the sound of the trees crunching; the snapping of branches to the rear.

Marauders!

Without thinking, he knelt by Alissa and took her pistol. He would fight them to the death but they wouldn't take her alive. Not while he could breathe.

He had seen what they did to women.

He cocked her pistol, pressed the muzzle next to her forehead and started to pull the trigger.

"No! TC! No!" The voice was familiar. He had heard it before, in the desert, begging him to leave him and save himself.

"Life in the biome . . . " Puhaly had said, *" . . . is better than death in the desert!"*

The pistol lowered. Creighton sagged and felt the powerful arms of Puhaly wrap him in a cocoon of strength.

Then he fell into the blackness of unconsciousness.

★★★★★★★★★★★★★

PART FOUR
STAGING

★★★★★★★★

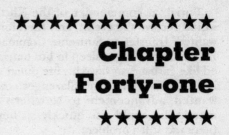

★★★★★★★★★★★★★
Chapter
Forty-one
★★★★★★★

0800.

General Hans Burril stood outside his tent at Northern Task Force headquarters, watching Slazenger as she strutted around the prize she had captured from the Americans. There was no concealing her joy; rarely did one express joy in this hellish part of the world. Not even when there was victory. He was struck by the fact that she was acting childishly, zealously pointing out the various parts of the aircraft which were a total mystery to him.

"This is where the operator sits." She climbed up the side of Thunder One and stood over the cockpit. She didn't understand the function of the array of instrumentation embedded in the instrument console, but she knew that in time others might determine their function.

"Damn the bastards," Burril snorted. He was referring to the inhabitants of the biosphere; the scientists who had managed to erase many forms of technology from the computers after the biosphere had been overthrown by the ancestors of Burril and Slazenger.

Flight was nonexistent in the Marauder society. But Burril could see how this might change now that there was a piece of machinery that could be duplicated. Duplication had been turned into an art form by the Marauder technicians.

Burril, as commander of the Northern Task Force, would receive the credit, and therefore receive what he wanted: transfer to Supreme Command Headquarters. He would no longer sleep in hot tents, eat food that tasted like garbage, or have his life put at risk by the advancing MNF element. And Slazenger could have what she wanted: advancement to Northern Task Force command. She could rise quickly, as her father had. But there was still a problem.

"The machine will be duplicated and provide an excellent advantage in the field. There remains the fact we need an operator. You have offered as much a problem as you have a solution."

Slazenger flushed with anger. "Our people can learn to operate the machine."

Burril didn't appear convinced. "But time, major. Time is against us. We are being driven back by the advancing Americans and Europeans." He waved his arm around the area. "In the last year we have lost all the territory and outposts we secured in a matter of months. Our present strategy, to kill all the inhabitants of the area therefore denying the use of their services to the Americans, is our only means of slowing their advance. That will be made more difficult now that they have machines that fly. We will not be able to move freely, or operate in the clear with such ease."

"We can learn to operate the machine," she insisted again, her words burning like acid.

Burril rubbed his square-shaped chin. His face was weathered, as though carved from the sun-baked hide of an animal. His hazel eyes moved slowly, but his mind was turning over a thought he had considered an hour after her arrival from an all-night march to deliver the aircraft to his headquarters.

Burril turned to one of his junior officers. "Bring the prisoner."

Slazenger climbed down from Thunder One.

"What prisoner?" She knew prisoners were rarely

taken. If at all, they were interrogated and executed within hours of capture.

Five minutes later, a group of soldiers appeared dragging a man whose hands and legs were bound with handcuffs and chains. Burril looked at the man as he was thrown to the ground at the general's feet. The man's face was badly swollen from the beating he had suffered through the night as interrogators wrung from him the answers they wanted.

Burril pointed at the man, telling Slazenger, "He came to our camp last night. He was once the leader of a group to the north. The damn fool was captured by the Americans."

Slazenger looked at the man. "Why is he still alive? That is treason. He should be shot."

Burril's face softened into a thin smile. "He has lived with the Americans for nearly a year. He was their prisoner. He has learned their ways. I think he can solve the problem of the operator."

Slazenger looked surprised. "How?"

Burril pulled the man to his feet. A stream of blood was dried on the side of his cheek where a boot had split open his eyebrow. There was hatred in his eyes that made Burril feel uncomfortable.

"You told me last night you had escaped from the Americans. That you hate the Americans." It wasn't a question.

Benhaddou pulled himself upright, taking on an air of pride. "I did escape. I rode the fast train through the American lines and stole a motorcycle. Your patrol found me and brought me here. I thought I was among friends. I can see I am not."

Burril nodded at the chains. An officer removed the steel cuffs from his wrists and the chains running from the cuffs to his ankles.

"Friendship must be earned. If you know the Americans as well as you claim . . . you will be rewarded." Burril took Benhaddou by the arm and led him toward his tent. He motioned for Slazenger to follow.

An hour later, Benhaddou left the tent. He was not under guard. He was given food, clothing, and weapons.

More importantly, to him, he was given freedom. And the opportunity to settle an old account.

★★★★★★★★★★★★★★

Chapter
Forty-two

★★★★★★★★

Two days had passed since Creighton had been recovered by Falken and the crew of the Chariot. His muscles still ached but he was in good shape. Breen was not as fortunate. She had lapsed in and out of consciousness from the poison of the spear. Creighton had not returned her to the rear for fear the journey overland to the train might worsen her condition. Besides, there was still another need she might have to fulfill if they were to recover Thunder One.

"What you're suggesting is insane, young captain." Roman Standish had arrived the night before with Shoemaker and the crew assigned to assemble the GroundStar station on the ridge separating the two valleys. "You haven't reconnoitered the area, and from what you've told me that would mean travelling fifty miles or more into the heart of enemy territory. I doubt Colonel Clayton would approve such a plan."

Creighton was sitting at a folding table beside the Chariot. Puhaly, Felot, and Armbrust were standing beside him. A map was spread out on the table.

"Falken is reconning the area to the south. He's taken a light recon team consisting of one MBT and his IFV. He should return late tonight with the intelligence we'll need."

"How will you fly the aircraft out? The pilot is still ill."

On the map, Creighton ran a finger from the valley

to the south. "Colonel Clayton is en route to our location at this moment. I doubt I have to tell you he's more
than a little pissed off about the loss of Thunder One.
Frankly, he told me to find the aircraft and either make
recovery—or destroy the aircraft."

"That'll mean a direct attack on the Marauder forces.
That'll be suicide," Roman argued.

Creighton grinned and stretched, massaging the sore
muscles of his neck as he explained his plan.

"Not necessarily. The aircraft is armed with a destructive mechanism that can be operated with an electronic
transmitter." He took a black transmitter from his jacket
pocket.

"The device will have been removed. You said yourself that the aircraft didn't explode when the Marauders
opened the cockpit."

Creighton shrugged. "There's a backup. Captain
Breen told me during our escape. She said the device is
armed and detonated in the same manner as the destruct
devices on our MBT's. We just have to get close."

"How close?" asked Roman.

"Eight hundred yards."

"My God! That's only a half mile."

"That's correct. Which means we'll have to make the
attack at night. We can go to stealth and chameleon, hit
the outer perimeter, and recover or detonate."

"You're suggesting a full-scale attack. Against what
amounts to a full division. Or larger. Our forces aren't
ready for such an encounter. That's been the purpose of
Clayton's OPLAN-3. To gradually encroach using pacified and trained indigenous hostiles."

Creighton looked at Armbrust. "We came here to
fight, Roman. Not to be diplomatic. The Marauders are
systematically erasing the indigenous population before
we can reach the area. If this scorched-earth policy con-
tinues, we'll have nothing to pacify and train. It's time
we took this program on the road."

"The odds are overwhelming."

"Our MBT's can take on six opponents at a time. They have us in numbers, but we have them in technology and training. Mike's squadron and mine can handle one division. We proved that last year on the eastern flank."

"You had the support of the Iron Horse and a fully equipped MNF armored squadron."

"We can beat them."

Roman shook his head; his long hair danced about his shoulders. He walked off toward the electronic animal pen that had been erected. He wanted to hear the sounds of Africa; the old Africa.

Not the sound of new Africa. The sound of war.

★★★★★★★★★★★★★★

Chapter
Forty-three

★★★★★★★

The animal reserve began less than a mile from where the armored units sat in bivouac. Though the area was designated off-limits, the sounds and smells of the animals drifted to the bivouac, permeating the air and leaving no doubt as to their location.

On the hill overlooking the reserve, Ibo sat mesmerized by the sight of the two White Rhinos. Adam had taken to the smell of the valley as though he had been born and raised in the bush. Eve was more timid. She would wander from her module inside an electronic force field determined by the sensors, which the rhinos shared, then return to the feeding stall.

The electronic control range was tight at the moment, which was necessary to keep the rhinos from intruding on the others' areas. But it allowed them to see and smell each other, acclimating them to each other as well as to the climate and landscape. The fields would gradually be extended over a period of time as the animals grew to recognize the boundaries of their new habitat.

Ibo knew nothing of the collars that made the animals prisoners in his valley; he understood none of this, even when explained by Shona.

Shona and Neshu had begun to form a friendship that did not go unnoticed by Dr. Peterson. She was taking blood samples from an anesthetized gorilla male when the two Africans came into the tent where she had

140

established her headquarters.

Neshu appeared nervous, which Dr. Peterson found unusual. The chieftess was not the sort to display emotion, especially embarrassment. Shona spoke for her.

"Neshu wishes to thank you for your kindness the other day."

Jean smiled at the tall woman. She sensed there was more. "Is that all?"

Shona now appeared embarrassed. He was the kind of man accustomed to taking what he wanted; fighting to hold onto what he had.

"The water that smells of sweetness. And the paint you put on her mouth. These are things she wished to thank you for . . . and to know if there are more. That she might find for herself."

Jean now understood. "Perfume and lipstick." She went to a canvas bag she carried at all times. From the bag she removed a small bottle of clear liquid and a tube. She sat Neshu at a folding chair and ran a streak of the lipstick over her lips. Next she dabbed the perfume beneath each of Neshu's ears. The fragrance caught Shona's attention. The redness of her lips made him smile.

"Here." She gave Neshu the tube and bottle. "Tell her to put both on each morning—" She stopped, looking at the flashing in Shona's eyes, then added, "Or whenever she wishes to please a man."

Shona explained. Neshu bowed respectfully, then they walked off together.

Roman entered at that moment. He was surprised by the Equinox Woman's appearance.

"My, my. There certainly must be something in the air." He grinned at Jean. "The animals aren't the only creatures in this valley that are starting to show signs of mating."

Jean laughed. "She's changing, Roman. A few days ago she despised men and all outsiders. Now she's starting to become one of the group. It's amazing what a little kindness can do."

Roman shook his head. "Kindness. A commodity too

rare on our planet. Perhaps one day it will return. God! I hate this violence."

Jean stared past him to Shona and Neshu. They were watching a pair of ostriches jump and dance in the early stages of the mating ritual.

"I'm going to ask Neshu to stay with us on the reserve. She has a natural love for animals. I think it would be good for her."

"And for you, my dear. A woman needs the company of women as well as men. I think it's a good idea. But what about communicating?"

"I'll teach her English. She's very bright. I think she will learn quickly."

"And the old man?"

Jean rubbed her palms together. Through the opening of the tent she could see Ibo squatting on the side of a hill, his club across his lap, watching the animals as though they were children. "He owns this valley. He's already a part of the team."

1000.

Falken had dismounted at the first sign of Marauder activity. The telltale sign of treadmarks in the dirt and the deep grooves from extended traffic told him he was close to some sort of encampment. He had left the MBT and his fighting vehicle in a camouflaged defensive posture. The terrain was rugged, rolling hills covered with trees; it was new to him, but he felt comfortable moving through the bush, pausing to listen for more noise.

Noise. That was what always gave away the Marauder position. The gas guzzlers relied on petrol, rather than solar power, marking their location by the sound of groaning engines and the thick black smoke from their exhausts.

Reaching a hill, he put the binoculars to his eyes and scanned a large clearing that spread out between two high ridges. The camp was garrisoned with what he thought were more than 200 tanks. Leopards. The old-style tank first developed by the Europeans in the twentieth century.

Then he saw what he was looking for: the airplane sat on its squat legs at the very center of the camp. Four guards walked monotonously around the strange-looking craft.

He was about two miles from the outer perimeter; too far away to activate the detonator. Any attempt on the aircraft would require the soldiers to push closer, exposing them to the guns of the Marauders.

That was when he saw a tall, black figure strutting through the camp as though he were the commander. Falken's lips tightened. He looked at his rifle, and though he was too far away, he knew he couldn't shoot, even if he wanted to.

He pulled back, eased his way to the two vehicles and mounted up. Taking the microphone, he transmitted into the recorder in the instrument console.

He spoke for several minutes, detailing the complete layout of the camp. His last words were spoken with particular distaste.

"In the camp, I saw someone else. Benhaddou!"

Chapter Forty-five

There was no missing the agitation in Colonel Clayton's features or voice. He stepped down from an MBT and walked directly toward the hospital tent erected by Creighton's medical unit. He passed by TC as though he didn't exist. Inside, he saw the bed holding the ward's single patient.

Captain Breen was sitting up, now showing less sign of the devastating effect of the poison. She looked tired; her eyes were swollen, but her hair was neatly combed.

Clayton sat on the edge of the bed. Creighton stood behind him, saying nothing.

"You're feeling better?"

She nodded. "I'm ready to return to duty."

Clayton looked at TC. "Duty with what? Your aircraft is now in the hands of the enemy. I'm sending you back to Base Camp One as soon as you're able. We have communications link-up with the United States now that GroundStar has been established at Base Camp One. I've requested another aircraft be sent. Your director has approved. Frankly, I wanted another pilot sent as well. He said you're the only one who knows the operation of the aircraft and the weapons system."

She seemed to take delight in that fact. "I'm here to fly, colonel. What happened was a risk of war. You know that, sir."

"War's ass, young lady. You took a highly sophisticat-

ed piece of equipment and exposed yourself and the aircraft to unnecessary risk. If you're going to stay in this
command you're going to have to obey orders. And use
the brains you have. Otherwise . . . pilot or not . . . you'll
be on the next ship back to the U.S. Is that understood?"

She saluted.

Clayton stood and left, followed by TC.

"I ought to put you in the goddamned brig!"

TC replied, "Yes, sir."

"Christ. How could you do something that stupid?"

TC stopped. He aimed a sharp index finger at the
AfriKorps C in C. "What do you mean? You sent her out
here with that contraption. What did you expect? I used
her and the machine in a perfectly legitimate military
mode."

"And got both of your asses shot out of the sky the
first time you encountered the enemy. Who—as you
may know—now possess the damned airplane. President
Dawson personally chewed my ass out for nearly an hour
when he learned what had happened. Jesus, TC. What
were you thinking?"

"I was thinking I might recon by air. That's the mission of Thunder One."

Clayton placed his helmet on his head, ordering as
he walked off, "Assemble all your officers in one hour.
We have a briefing. I want every available piece of equipment and personnel ready to roll by sundown."

"A night attack?"

"I have something else planned. I received Falken's
report on the way into your camp. He says the enemy
encampment is division size. Our tactics will have to
change somewhat. I'll explain at the briefing. And
there's something else."

"What's that?"

"He saw something else of interest."

"What?"

"That sonofabitch Benhaddou."

Creighton felt his blood chill. "So the bastard reached their lines. I'm not surprised."

"Get busy, son." Clayton started to walk away, then stopped and asked, "Where's Roman?"

Chapter
Forty-six

★★★★★★★★

1300.

Benhaddou threw his leg over the seat of the stolen motorcycle and pressed the switch that started the engine. The machine ran off a battery pack that was good for nearly one hundred hours. He figured that would give him plenty of energy to complete his mission before the engine died.

He had learned how to operate the machine while in prison, reading from the library books provided for him by his jailers. They had sharpened the knife that would open their veins, he told himself as he streaked from the large encampment.

A deal had been struck and he would keep his end of the bargain. Not that he was honorable. He was practical. The AfriKorps would hunt him like an animal. Caught between two opposing forces, he would have to do the bidding of the Marauders or return to the dangers that waited in the countryside.

He had grown accustomed to certain benefits of the two factions: food that tasted good, pure water, and women that didn't have sores on their belly. He wasn't certain which was more pleasing.

He took the motorcycle cross-country, through the notch in the hills that would lead along the coastal savannah grasslands to where the valley of the Equinox tribes had once been.

To where he would find the two things he had to have if he were to survive: the pilot and Creighton.

★★★★★★★★★★★★★

Chapter
Forty-seven

★★★★★★★

1400.

Falken and the MBT reached Clayton's headquarters as the briefing was about to begin. Officers were filing into the large tent; one reminded Falken that he was to report immediately.

"Fuck them. I smell like one of those giraffes," Reno said to himself. He went directly to a shower stall, turned on the water, and stood there for several minutes.

The briefing could wait. He was hot. Tired. And he wasn't certain his recon had provided enough answers to the many questions still remaining.

He sensed Clayton was going to attack the enemy. A well-entrenched enemy dug-in behind deep bunkers and surrounded by minefields. That went against the grain of the open-field fighting AfriKorps had trained for.

Their technology was designed to fight on the move, denying themselves as targets, and certainly against a smaller force. They would have sixty tanks against more than two hundred. Five hundred troops against as many as three thousand.

He stepped from the stall and peeled off his uniform, opened a clothing packet, and dressed in clean fatigues.

Strapping on his pistol belt as he walked, he reached the tent where Clayton's voice echoed from inside.

"Intel gathered from Lieutenant Falken's reconnaissance mission shows a large, well-equipped enemy armored unit of division size with supporting infantry.

Additionally, the enemy have our aircraft secured at the center of the perimeter." He propped a rough map of the camp on an easel. The officers could see the camp was surrounded by a minefield that lay in front of a barbed-wire fence. Within the fence infantry positions were supported by tanks; at the center, a ring of tanks surrounded the command headquarters and the aircraft.

Armbrust released a long whistle. He leaned to TC and whispered, "We're going to earn our pay on this one, old buddy."

TC nodded. He knew the MBT's could hold their own against the opposing tanks; the heavier price would be paid by the ground troops fighting inside the perimeter.

Creighton raised his hand. "That will cost us a lot of lives, colonel. A direct attack sounds unnecessarily hazardous."

"Be patient, young captain," the colonel replied. "We're not going to attack directly . . . or indirectly."

Clayton held a pointer to the map and traced the southern escape route that led to the next valley. "The Marauder commander has no doubt given himself a way out in the event of attack. Or a route to bring in reinforcements."

At that moment, Creighton began to understand where the C in C's strategy was leading.

Clayton touched the escape route leading through the mountains. "Captain Armbrust's Panther squadron will move to the south, establishing a block at this point. Captain Creighton's Lion squadron will surround the encampment."

That's when someone whispered aloud the word that defined the colonel's plan.

"Siege!"

Clayton grinned. "Precisely. A siege." He ran the pointer along the low-lying foothills that formed a horseshoe on all flanks except to the south. "Lion squadron will move into position in these hills, taking up a full defilade posture. With our guns trained down, and our tanks protected by the terrain, we won't give them anything to shoot at."

"What if they attack us?" an officer asked.

"Our intelligence personnel have developed what we consider to be a good characterization of the Marauders' offensive doctrine. Our encounter with the Marauders last year on the eastern front indicates a mentality to utilize wave tactics, much like the Soviet tactics of the twentieth century. If we have our guns trained down on them, they won't be able to use this tactic. They won't be able to get out of the encampment."

The officers studied the positioning of the tanks in the camp and understood.

Creighton whispered to Armbrust, "They're bunched up tighter than a frog's ass underwater. Their tanks won't be able to move in any direction except straight ahead. And that'll be a traffic nightmare."

Clayton continued. "Defensively speaking, wave tactics generally dictate a strong outer perimeter and weak inner perimeter for rapid deployment. According to Falken's report they have 80 percent of their personnel and equipment on the outer two echelons and grouped tight, depriving them of mobility inside the perimeter. Essentially, by training our fire on them—and keeping them buttoned up in their own tank pits—they won't be able to break out and engage us beyond the minefields. In essence, my counterpart has created his own perfect trap. He can't come out—and he'll be destroyed systematically if he stays inside."

"How do we recover the aircaft?" asked one officer.

"Once engagement begins we will concentrate heavy firepower on three key points. By punching a hole through any of the three points we can send in a unit to the interior and either recover the aircraft or destroy it where it sits."

Colonel Creighton checked his watch. "We will deploy under cover of darkness. Our night vision and stealth capability will get us to the enemy encampment before they know we're there. Gentlemen, they'll eat sour pork for breakfast. You are excused to ready your units. I want the two squadron commanders to remain behind for a personal briefing. That is all."

Creighton and Armbrust remained and listened to Clayton's two final orders.

"Captain Armbrust, you will have to hold down the south gate of the valley. Nothing comes in . . . nothing goes out. I don't know what kind of enemy relief may lay to the south, but I doubt there's much that can assist once we begin the siege."

He turned to Creighton. "Captain, you get the tricky end of the stick. You will form a special operations unit consisting of one MBT and three IFV's with full infantry and heavy weapons complement to make the run to the interior of the perimeter. Additionally, you will have one lorry with a winch to put the aircraft onto the lorry and transport it from the camp."

TC shook his head. "I can take my MBT and Reno will lead the three IFV's. It's the lorry that presents the greatest risk. Whoever drives will be a sitting duck. Not to mention the crew that'll hoist the aircraft onto the lorry."

"It's a risky business, captain," Clayton replied. "Find the right men. You can check with the motor pool. I'm sure there's enough men there to volunteer."

Creighton and Falken saluted as the colonel walked away.

"That's a tall order, TC."

Creighton walked off mumbling, "Let's go to the motor pool and see if we can find someone suicidal."

Chapter
Forty-eight

★★★★★★★★

1400.

Puhaly was straddling the long barrel of the Chariot's 120mm cannon, working the cleaning pole through it. Fergus was underneath checking the engine and the solar batteries. There was a low-key attitude in the camp, as was usual before men go into battle. Talk was low; laughter was light and nervous. Traditional grab-ass was almost nonexistent as the men's thoughts began to shift to the business at hand. Commanders kept their men busy, even though some details were trivial; an age-old remedy for keeping minds from focusing on death.

Puhaly was whistling softly, an old tune from the twentieth century, "I left My Heart In San Francisco."

He stopped, and leaning over, called to Fergus Felot. "You ever been in a siege?"

Felot replied in a voice that sounded like an echo issuing from beneath the Chariot, "Not what you would call a real siege. A one-day affair in DESFOR. We had a group of hostiles pinned down in the mountains. They were holed up in caves. The little buggers died to the last man, woman, and child. But I'll tell you one thing . . . there's noise, boy-o. More noise than that valley will ever hear again. And the poor devils on the receiving end will think they're living in the trash can of Hell."

"Yeah. That's what I understand. If the HEAT rounds don't get them, the noise blows out their eardrums.

Equilibrium goes to hell. Gunners can't sight accurately. They start shooting each other in the ass."

"That's the way of the siege. Noise. Cannon fire. Rocket launchers. Machine guns. Gut-wrenching, ball-twisting noise. All day. Into the night. No sleep. No food. No rest. The buggers'll be ready to lay down their arms by morning. Unless, of course, their commander's a maniac."

"It'll be a Fourth of July fireworks the likes of which we may never see again." Puhaly grinned. "I wonder how many of the bastards I'll kill!"

He slid along the barrel and dropped into his gunner's chair. Pressing a button on the console he saw he was armed with twenty-four HEAT rounds and twenty-four SABOT rounds. "I'll drop off twelve SABOT and replace with 12 HEAT," he said aloud.

Then he sighted through the laser rangefinder at a tank fifty meters to the front. The digital readout matched precisely his calculation and he knew the sight was dead on the money. Next he checked the smoke dispenser, making certain the canisters were loaded to the maximum.

Ammunition for the co-axials and the 30mm was topped out. Checking the first-aid kit, he reminded himself to pick up morphine from the medic; he had used a Syrette on Captain Breen. Finally, he checked the halon gas canisters in the automatic fire suppression system (AFSS) that would automatically fill the interior of the tank should there be a fire.

"This bitch is ready!" he whispered to the gunsight.

At that moment, Fergus pulled himself through the floor escape hatch. The sides of his green eyes were etched with crowfoot wrinkles; his red hair had a slight gray tinge, but he showed no fear.

Ribald's Chariot was ready for war!

Chapter
Forty-nine

★★★★★★★

Creighton found Alissa sitting on the edge of her bunk, trying to put on her boots. When she pitched forward he caught her before she fell to the floor. He held her for a moment, then gently lifted her back on the cot.

"Where did you think you were going?" he asked.

"To find Colonel Clayton. You'll need me when you recover Thunder One."

Creighton shook his head. "You wouldn't make it through the door of this tent. Back you go. Lay down and behave."

She laid back and he found that he was still holding her hand. Cool. Soft. The way he remembered his wife's hands. He flushed as she stared at the laced fingers and released his grip.

"What time are you leaving?" she asked.

"Eight o'clock. Silent march is the order from the C in C."

"Is he going?"

Creighton laughed. "You can say what you want about Colonel Clayton, but he's a soldier's soldier. He'll go. I'm surprised he didn't assign himself the task of leading the special ops unit into the camp."

She sat up, wincing slightly as the pain from the wound stung her body. "You have a lot of respect for him."

"In some ways. In other ways I don't. You know what I mean."

"Silver?"

TC nodded and looked away. He didn't see Alissa reach into her canvas tote bag. She took out an envelope and handed it to him. "I want you to read this."

She gave him the letter. He instantly recognized the handwriting of his dead wife. He began reading the letter.

Dear Alissa,

It's with excitement and enthusiasm that I write you to tell you I am going to be married to that young man we both liked so much as children. Abraham Creighton. You wouldn't know him now since he's grown into a tall, handsome man with dark hair and warm, bedroom brown eyes.

We'll be married in a week, before we leave for our honeymoon in Africa!

That's right. Africa! Can you imagine? I was always the one frightened of anything new and mysterious.

I don't know what waits for us there, but we'll have each other and many of our friends from the Vegas Biosphere will be going along, especially Abe's military unit. For that I'm glad. Glad that he's staying in the military. It's where he belongs. Where his heart and soul lie.

Can you see him as a farmer! Or me as a farmer's wife?

We were going to join the Pioneer Program and resettle on a farm in the central part of the region, but Colonel Clayton, the commander of the military unit now preparing to deploy to Africa, requested I be assigned to the unit. Of course, that meant Abe had to stay in the military and deploy to Africa with his tank squadron.

He was furious! Frankly, I'm grateful to Colonel Clayton. Abe despises him for assigning me to his unit, but I know there was more to his decision than having me as a physician and Abe as one of his squadron commanders. There's something deeper between the two; something Abe has never quite understood.

He's given Abe and I the opportunity to see a new and exciting part of the world. A part of the world no American has seen since the Cataclysm. More importantly, Colonel Clayton has given us the chance to be together in a great adventure where we'll have only each other and no one else.

For that, I will always be indebted to Colonel Clayton.

Which reminds me to discuss another, more personal matter. Should something happen to me I want you to somehow find Abe. Find him, Alissa, and be there for me. He will be hurt and angry, and that could cause greater damage than any enemy might ever cause.

Remind him I would rather have died at his side in Africa than have watched him die a slow death as a farmer.

He's a soldier. Not a farmer. And I'm a soldier's wife!

The words stung . . . *I'm a soldier's wife!*

Creighton laid the letter on the cot and stood. His face was frozen into a mask; a mask that barely hid the pain he was feeling.

Without saying a word, he walked out of the hospital tent.

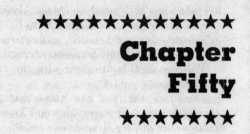

★★★★★★★★★★★★★★

Chapter
Fifty

★★★★★★★★

1600.

Dr. Paul Shoemaker stood on the ridge overlooking the valley. Below, the military units could be seen preparing for the forced night march that would lead to the next confrontation with the enemy from the south. Nearby, his GroundStar technicians were erecting the modular structure that would serve as a shelter for the communications equipment, the solar receptor that would provide the energy required to operate it, and the antennae for signal transmission and reception.

A signal unit from AfriKorps had been attached to Shoemaker's project; training was on-the-job for the most part, though the systems were not that difficult for the soldiers to understand.

Communications would now be linked from the point of the reserve to Base Camp One, nearly 1,000 miles away.

Since the module came in pre-fabbed sections, erection was simple and quick. The technicians had begun that morning after the site had been levelled the day before by an MBT utilizing a quick-attach plow blade.

Colonel Clayton had driven up the ridge with Roman Standish to oversee the final installation of the receivers for the microwave equipment.

"Installation should be complete by midnight, colonel. Then you'll have direct communication from this point to the United States via Alaska and the Soviet Union. Remarkable, don't you think?"

"About damned time," Clayton grunted, but Shoemaker knew the C in C was pleased.

"Will the signals interfere with the reserve animals?" asked Roman.

"Not in the slightest. The frequencies are on two separate wavelengths. The animals won't know we're here. Dr. Peterson has set her frequencies to allow the animals full freedom of the valley with the exception of the higher elevation on the ridgeline. There will be no interference."

Clayton studied the module. "Looks like a shiny giant tortoise."

Shoemaker beamed with pride. "The outer layer is most resilient. Barring a direct hit from an artillery round, the module can withstand a great deal of punishment."

Clayton looked up at the sky. Dark clouds were rolling in from the east. "What about electrical interference from thunderstorms? I'd hate to see this site turn into a lightning rod."

"Actually, lightning can be beneficial. The outer layer will glean the electrical static in the air and store the energy in the battery pods."

Clayton thought about the reason he came to see Shoemaker. "Is it possible to use your module to tap into another communications system?"

Shoemaker looked suspiciously at Clayton. "You're referring to the enemy's communications?"

"You're a quick study, Dr. Shoemaker. I want to be able to listen in on their frequencies . . . and transmit to their commo center. Is that possible?"

Shoemaker left without saying a word. He returned several minutes later carrying a small case similar to a briefcase. He opened it and motioned for Clayton to examine the contents.

"This is what I call GroundStar Forward Listening Post. FLP for short."

Shoemaker removed a small hemispherical disc that was supported by three fold-out legs. He snapped the legs into place and connected a battery pack concealed inside the briefcase. He held up a small headset that plugged directly into the side of the disc. Pointing at a digital display, he explained how the FLP operated.

"The FLP has a scanning device that can intercept frequencies from a distance of fifty miles, so long as there is no physical interruption."

"By that you mean terrain?"

"That's correct. Once scanning begins, transmissions can be intercepted, captured, and communications established along the same frequency."

"In other words, if we set up this gizmo near the enemy we can intercept their communications and listen to their conversations?"

"Intercept and listen . . . or communicate with them directly over their communications network."

Roman saw an immediate problem. "What about the language barrier? The Marauder language is different from ours."

Clayton grinned. "We have someone who can speak their language."

Then Roman remembered the man who spoke the strange language of the southern invaders. "Shona," he said.

"Shona can act as our intermediary. Our ears into their camp. We'll know every move they plan to make."

Roman thought of another aspect of the new means of communicating with the enemy. "You can also reason with the commander of the Marauders. Perhaps convince him of the futility of fighting once the siege begins."

Clayton shook his head. "That's not the priority. First priority is to destroy the Marauder division. We'll talk . . . but not until I'm certain there's no fight left in the bastards."

Clayton then closed up the briefcase and climbed

into his Landrover. He saluted Shoemaker, then waited for Roman to get in the jeep.

On the drive down the narrow road carved into the mountainside by the plow, Roman's thoughts returned to a conversation the two had had at Base Camp One.

"Do you want me to talk with Captain Creighton before your unit takes to the field?"

Clayton shook his head. "He has enough on his mind. That can wait until after the mission."

"You're taking a great chance either way."

"How's that?"

"When I tell him . . . he may become overwrought. Perhaps violent. You could lose what you hope to gain. If I don't tell him, and something happens to him during the mission . . . you'll have to spend the rest of your life wondering whether you made the right decision."

Clayton slowed to negotiate a narrow curve in the road. "Either way . . . it's the decision I've made."

"I still think you should not let him know the part about his father. That might be too much."

Clayton slammed on the brakes. He turned and faced the philosopher. "He has to know the truth. If not about me. Then about himself."

They drove off. Roman wasn't certain what would happen in the upcoming mission, but he knew that after the mission the greatest danger either TC or Clayton could face in their lives could destroy them both:

Truth!

Chapter
Fifty-one

★★★★★★★★

1800.

The armored column sat in formation like a great phalanx. In his MBT, Clayton, signified by the red pennant flying above the main hatch, was at the front of the two squadrons of high-tech armor. To the C in C's immediate rear was stationed the headquarters company composed of engineers, medics, and the lorry that would be used to carry Thunder One from inside the enemy camp.

Creighton and Armbrust sat at the lead of their squadrons on the flanks. Thirty MBT's with a full complement of IFV's formed the squadrons, with the exception of Falken, who was already out front running point patrol.

Clayton keyed the switch on his boom mike, ordering, "All units, advance slow."

The air stirred with the hum of the MBT's as the solar-powered machines pushed forward. Clayton's headquarters company took the lead, followed by Creighton's Lion squadron.

Panther squadron under Armbrust's command took up the rear. An hour later, as the chain of battle machines passed the west entrance to the valley of the Equinox, Armbrust's squadron swung east through the valley to make the eight-hour march through a series of mountain passes that would lead his tanks to the south flank of the enemy encampment.

In the briefing, Clayton had designated the mission *OPLAN Siege,* for Operational Plan Siege.

The Marauder valley was designated *Green Gate.*

Reports brought to him by Falken indicated the terrain was becoming more lush and green during the southern trek toward the tip of Africa. It was a good sign. Gone was the hot, arid desert. The thought of trees and tall grass gave the southern push a new vitality.

The men of AfriKorps knew they would see sights never seen by their ancestors, the men and women who lived in the biospheres during the Cataclysm, only to emerge and find sheer desolation.

More importantly, by destroying the Marauder division, Clayton felt the pacification of Quadrant Two could be facilitated in a short period of time. Then the thrust through the waist of Africa could begin. The push to the southern tip would be underway.

But first there was the battle in Green Gate!

★★★★★★★★★★★★★

PART FIVE
SIEGE!

★★★★★★★★

★★★★★★★★★★★★★

CHAPTER
FIFTY-TWO

★★★★★★★

Above the reserve, Dr. Peterson and Roman Standish stood on the site where GroundStar was nearly complete. They watched silently as the armored procession wound its way from the valley, then disappeared into the setting sun.

Dr. Peterson folded her arms around herself as a slight chill tickled the air. "How long will the mission take, Roman?"

Roman shrugged, replying, "Two hours . . . two days . . . two weeks. It depends on several factors. Most important the element of total surprise. If Clayton doesn't encounter enemy patrols and can move into position before the Marauders move out of the encampment, the siege will begin immediately."

"Is that possible? Total surprise? Can they avoid enemy patrols?"

"That's the key. Moving under cover of darkness, our MBT's can operate in stealth and chameleon mode and move undetected against the laser equipment of the enemy. The sheer boldness of the plan will take the enemy by surprise. Colonel Clayton figures that if there is contact, the enemy will suspect it's only a small patrol. Or a probe. The Marauder commander might send out a small platoon, but he wouldn't send out an entire division. It's the enemy assumption of security that Clayton is counting on. He doesn't believe the enemy commander would suspect an attack on such a large force."

"Now I can see the importance of the aircraft. If the aircraft hadn't been lost, Colonel Clayton would have airborne reconnaissance in the sky over the Marauder camp."

"That's true. Which reminds me . . . how is the pilot? Is she recovering?"

"She's doing quite well. Her temperature has dropped. The wound is still healing but her strength is returning. She should be out of the hospital in a few days, and up and about tomorrow."

Roman started to say something else, but he heard the sound of rocks tumbling down the hillside. Hoisting his toga, he walked toward the darkness where he heard the sound. He saw nothing. Attuning his ears to the night, he heard nothing.

Then he felt a sudden chill, as though the presence of something evil lurked nearby. Jean Peterson walked over to him.

"Did you hear something?"

Roman shrugged, saying, "It was probably nothing but loose rock falling. Come, my dear, let's see how much more work is required to get this GroundStar facility operational."

They disappeared into the module, where light momentarily bled from the open door. Darkness returned to the ridge.

There was the slightest movement in the rocks nearby. A tall figure, momentarily caught in the moonlight, cast a long shadow that stretched across the ground.

Then there was nothing.

★★★★★★★★★★★★★★
Chapter
Fifty-three
★★★★★★★

Ibo sat on the hillside below the GroundStar site. He had paid little attention to the war machines that moved almost soundlessly from the valley. He had sat watching the animals below. The sun was now gone, the moonlight pale, but it was bright enough for him to see something strange.

Rising, leaning on his club, he saw a shadowy figure moving through the thin veil of darkness below. The figure walked upright. A man.

Carefully, Ibo made his way down the hillside and into the camp. There was a sudden stir among the animals as the dark figure slinked quietly through the staging area where the animals were being held.

At night, the animals were held in their holding pens, allowing them more time to become accustomed to a darkened environment. It was the time of day Ibo loved most, when the animals were more receptive to human companionship. When he could get close to the animals. Touch them. Whisper words to them in a language their species had not heard in more than a century.

Following a path, he could see the figure pause at the tent of Dr. Peterson. Moments later, the figure moved east, toward the military detachment left in reserve.

That was where Ibo's old eyes failed him and he lost

sight of the stranger whose scent he followed like a lion tracking an antelope.

A noise stopped him suddenly. The animals could be heard. The frantic sound of hooves, of snorting bulls. Then he understood. The scent of the stranger was now lost to a more powerful smell: Smoke!

Fire!

★★★★★★★★★★★★★

Chapter
Fifty-four

★★★★★★★★

Less than a half mile away, the fire licked the black night like the breath from a dragon in a deep, dark cave. The smoke painted the horizon in a soft pall; the screams of animals echoed from the ground, rising, drifting on the wind that blew from the east.

Benhaddou grinned at his deception. He had been crafty, resourceful. He had watched the armored column leave the valley from his place of hiding not far from where the GroundStar site was located. He had crossed the mountain from the Equinox valley with relative ease aboard the stolen motorcycle.

Like a reptile slithering through the rocks, he had moved unnoticed past the old man he remembered from his trial. The man called Roman, who had requested that the American colonel give him a fair trial and not summary execution. Roman had requested that Benhaddou be placed in a jail cell for the rest of his life rather than be executed after the military tribunal had found him guilty.

He would have killed the old bastard minutes before were it not for his mission. He had only one thought—not of revenge—of success. Revenge would come at a later date!

The fire was the stroke of genius that was now pulling

most of the soldiers from their camp. Only a few remained.

He was watching them now, the guards walking their posts around the barbed wire strung to form the camp's outer perimeter. Kneeling in the darkness, he recalled the land mines used by the Americans to protect their camp surrounded by the sharp wire.

Quietly, he slipped off into the trees where he moved quickly among the tall saplings growing in the treeline not far from the camp. When he found the right sapling he removed his long knife and carefully began carving at the tree until he felt and smelled the sweet tree meat beneath the bark. His cutting motion was slow and methodical, and he took great care not to make noise.

When the tree shuddered and started to sway, he gripped the trunk, which was the size of his fist, and carefully eased the sapling to the ground.

Sweat was pouring from his forehead as he stripped away the smaller branches; finally, he cut away the top of the sapling until he was left with a pole ten feet long.

Carrying the pole, he walked, bent low, staying in the shadows of the treeline until he reached a point near the fence where the guards were now marching away from each other.

He took a deep breath, gripped the pole, and started running toward the fence. Reaching the point where he knew the minefield began, he ignored the fear that he might be blown to pieces. He thought of nothing except the five steps he would have to take to get through the minefield before he planted the pole in the ground and vaulted over the fence.

Benhaddou ran toward the minefield. He could only hope that luck would get him through as he started counting the five deadly steps through the minefield.

One. He felt his legs grow stronger.

Two. His knees drove high.

Three. His arms brought the pole back at his side.

Four. His arms carried the pole forward to a spot he saw at the edge of the fence.

Five! He planted the pole into the ground.

He had succeeded!

As the pole bent, he threw his weight forward, then pulled with all his strength. He straightened his legs toward the stars as he felt his body swing upward, where the highest strand of ribbon wire was just beneath his back. He swung his legs over the wire and extended his arms, allowing the pole to fall to the other side.

Then he felt his feet touch the earth; he rolled, snapped upright, and hurried for the shadow of a tent. That was when, in the moonlight, he recognized the faint emblem painted on the next tent.

A red cross.

Chapter Fifty-five

★★★★★★★★★

Ibo knelt by the smoldering remnants of the wildebeest *kraal*. He recalled hearing Shona explain to Dr. Peterson that it was the African name for "corral." The male wildebeest lay on its side. Its hide smelled foul from the fire that was slowly consuming what was left. The stench from the burned flesh was acrid. His nostrils stung, but he could still smell the scent of the man he knew started the inferno.

Roman Standish stood by another holding pen. His long toga was nearly black from the smoke that punished the air like the bats in Ibo's cave.

The Equinox Woman was the one for whom Ibo felt the most pain. She had lost everything, then found something new. Fresh. Now most of that was gone.

Walking through the *kraal*, Ibo heard a cry from Dr. Peterson. He hurried to the pen, his heart racing. He knew what the pen held but he couldn't think of anything. He could only hope. When he reached the *kraal*, his heart nearly stopped.

Dr. Peterson knelt on the ground, her hand extended to a quivering mass that writhed in agony. The loud, heavy snort from Adam, the bull White Rhino, snapped Ibo back to his senses.

Kneeling beside Dr. Peterson, he looked at her. Tears

streamed down her face. There was a look of anger on it that nearly equalled his.

He could not speak her language. Nor could she speak his. But their sadness—and hatred—seemed to bind them together, transcending barriers of verbal communication.

Ibo stood and raised his club to the sky. His nose thrust upward. He ran crazily around the area for several minutes until finally, he aimed the club to the east.

He grunted some long-lost battle cry and charged in the direction the scent of the murderer led him.

Chapter
Fifty-six

★★★★★★★★

0200.

Voices filtered through the jungle; murmurs that made
no sense to Reno Falken. Kneeling by a strange-looking
bush, he looked hard through the trees, where the faint
glow of firelight flickered green through his night
vision goggles. Occasionally he would see a soldier
stand at the fire, toss some wood onto the flame, then
disappear, hidden by the foliage.

He crept closer, until he could see the clearing. He
recognized the position as a listening post; an early
warning site to flash to the division any advance by
AfriKorps. The men appeared lax in their discipline,
which he didn't find surprising. Carefully, he backed
out in a crouch, erasing his footprints as he retraced his
steps.

Ten minutes later, he reached his IFV. Shona was
one of the men waiting at the rear of the vehicle. Falken
went to the radio and put on his headphones. He
pressed the key button on his boom mike and whispered, "I have an enemy listening post 200 meters to
the front. One Leopard tank and two light infantry vehicles. Approximately one dozen infantry troops. The
troops appear bedded down. Four walking guards. One
light machine-gun position. The gun position is

176

unmanned. Request further instructions."

From the command post in his MBT, Clayton's voice replied, "Take out the LP. Take prisoners for interrogation."

Falken's IFV was manned by a driver and twelve light infantry soldiers. "Light fighters" they were called. Crack hit-and-run troops skilled in travelling light, and close combat; silent and deadly.

Falken drew the layout of the LP in the dirt. He gave instructions to his men. One carried a rifle with a silencer threaded on the muzzle. A night vision sniper scope was mounted on top of the rifle.

"Jess, take out the walking guards with the sniper rifle. I'll take the rest of the men and work through the bivouac area. They're sleeping on the ground. We're going to play a little one-on-one. Shona . . . you take the Leopard. Come in from the top. Drop this in first."

Falken handed Shona a stun grenade. Then he gave him a small Syrette. Shona sealed the needle on the Syrette by pressing the plunger. The he withdrew the plunger, leaving a small drop of the antistun serum bubbling at the point of the needle. He pressed the needle to his forearm and worked the serum into his bloodstream.

Falken looked at the sniper. "You start the party when you're in position. We'll need sixty seconds after we break off."

Removing a sharp knife from his scabbard, Falken looked around as the light fighters took out their knives. "No noise unless absolutely necessary." The driver and one soldier remained at the IFV as the deadly light fighters slipped silently through the darkness.

Reaching the clearing, Shona broke away from the others and moved in the direction of the Leopard.

The sniper began counting to sixty as he stepped into

the camouflage of a bush and raised his rifle. He sighted on the first sentry, then swung to the second, the third, the fourth.

When the sniper reached sixty, he squeezed off the first round, then the second, the third, the fourth. The silencer reduced the roar of the automatic rifle to a sound similar to a child coughing. Four soft, yet distinct coughs alerted Falken that the guards were being killed. He looked at the perimeter to see the first man pitch backward as the bullet tore through his head. The second guard clutched his throat and dropped silently to his knees. The third somersaulted backward, landing in a clump. The fourth spun wildly to the ground, his weapon clattering to the soft dirt. The scenario was over within 2.5 seconds. During the sniper's wait of sixty seconds, Falken's men had circled the bivouac to where the infantry lay sleeping. Hearing and seeing the guards drop was the signal for the light fighters to begin their deadly mission. Like stalking tigers, they crept toward each human clump lying in the forefront of the fire.

Falken stopped as one soldier rolled over; when he began snoring again, the deadly advance continued. Reaching the first soldier, Falken gripped the man beneath the chin, wrenched the head upright, and plunged the blade through the throat until he felt the point strike bone. With a hard jerk, Falken opened the man's throat with the ease of slicing a tomato. A rush of air was followed by a gurgle, then the death spasm began. Falken held the man pinned to the ground with his body weight until he heard the man's bowels release. The same sound erupted around Falken as he heard his light fighters strip the life from the enemy soldiers. Six seconds later, the twelve enemy soldiers lay bleeding to death; their throats slit from ear to ear; carotid arteries slashed open.

Falken looked to the Leopard. He froze as he saw a

head rise through the opened turret. Suddenly, a search-light was on, framing the AfriKorps soldiers in its brilliance. Through the illumination, Falken saw the Marauder spin the light machine gun mounted on the turret.

The metallic ring of the weapon's cocking lever loading a round into the chamber ate through Falken's guts. He saw the barrel level on him.

He closed his eyes and heard a scream. One of my men! Then there was silence.

Fighting the fear, Falken rose to his feet, drawing his weapon. He was prepared to die. Shona stood in the turret, his arm around the neck of the enemy tank commander. He had seen the man's head pop through the turret as he had begun creeping onto the hull. The lights had blinded him for a moment, but he had reached and grabbed the soldier as he was preparing to fire the machine gun. The scream had come when the soldier's neck snapped beneath Shona's great strength. Falken raised his pistol, taking aim at the figure, which was hazy through the punishing glare of the search light. His finger was about to close around the trigger when he heard Shona's voice shout, "AfriKorps!" Falken saw Shona drop the body and pull the pin of the grenade with the same motion.

Inside the tank, the driver and gunner had been awakened by the scream. They had started out of the Leopard when there was a loud explosion. A burst of white light filled the interior of the tank.

There was a tremendous buzzing in their ears, and the white flash of light froze their eyeballs in their sockets; froze their brains in their skulls. They could do nothing except watch in frozen terror as a huge black man dressed in robe and turban slid into the interior.

Each of the soldiers felt a crushing blow from his powerful fist. The ringing in their ears stopped as they fell into the swirling tempest of unconsciousness.

Chapter Fifty-seven

★★★★★★★

0200.

Colonel Clayton sat in a folding chair at the side of his MBT. Pop-out commo centers were integrated into the hulls of the MBT's, allowing for communication with infantry troops, or for use by the tankers when the MBT's were sitting in bivouac. The coolness and openess of the night felt good to Clayton, but nothing could have equalled the news he was receiving from Falken.

"We've got the bastards!" The C in C clapped his hands loudly, then cursed his enthusiasm as he reminded himself he was presently in or near enemy territory.

Creighton stood nearby, looking tired from the forced night march through rough terrain and into unknown territory.

Puhaly and Felot were asleep on the ground beside the Chariot. The rest of Lion squadron was deployed on the flanks.

Clayton motioned TC to the map.

"Shona has questioned one of the soldiers. Apparently, there are a series of outlying LP's strung along the main entrance into Green Gate. We'll have to run a gauntlet. Very dangerous. The element of surprise will be gone."

TC ran his finger along the long crack-back ridge

that rimmed the north of the valley. "What about LP's in this area?"

Clayton shook his head and pulled out his last bottle of scotch whiskey given to him by Eliason, the American scientist. He poured two drinks. "That's their weakness. Their equipment can't operate effectively in the rough terrain. Too many breakdowns, according to the prisoner. The enemy commander, a nasty bastard named Burril, has ordered the valley plugged and sealed . . . but the mountain ridgeline is open."

Creighton understood what the C in C had in mind. "You want us to go over the mountain ridgeline under cover of darkness!"

"That's our only choice. Which means we have four hours to get our equipment over the ridge and into position to begin the siege."

"That's impossible. It's not far in the distance, maybe ten miles. But it may as well be on the moon. Our MBT's are not designed to fight in that kind of terrain. They're open-field fighting machines. There's no road . . . not even a trail. The rocks will chew our treads to pieces. We'll become stranded."

Clayton straightened his shoulders. He wasn't accustomed to an officer questioning his decisions. "You may have a problem with that order, Captain Creighton. But you will follow the order. Is that understood?"

Creighton said nothing, but the C in C saw the muscles tighten in his jaw. TC was leaning over the map, a glimmer in his eye.

"Where did you get this map, colonel?"

Clayton thought for a moment. "Maps of the continent are reproduced from maps that were catalogued by the government before the Cataclysm. Why?"

TC pointed at the ridgeline. On each side of the mountain range separating their present location from the valley designed Green Gate was a continuous black line with smaller, uniform perpendicular cross lines.

"The black line . . . with the smaller cross lines evenly spaced. Do you know what they represent?"

Clayton looked at the black line. His eyes went to the legend at the corner of the map. He found the proper symbol. "I believe it represents a railroad track."

"Yes. A railroad track. I remember the engineer from the Iron Horse showing me the different map symbols."

Clayton examined the railroad tracks. He noticed there was a crevice in the middle of the mountain where the black line was interrupted by the mountain range. "If there was a railroad track over the mountain, it would be impossible to get past this location. There would have to have been a bridge at this location to cross this crevice. I doubt if it's still standing. If it is standing—it'll be damned unsafe for our equipment."

Creighton grinned from ear to ear. "Not a bridge over the mountain, colonel. Look at these two symbols on each side of the mountain. Where the tracks end."

Clayton saw another symbol. "Looks strange. Similar to a U with the uprights bent outward." He looked at the legend. "There's nothing here to indicate its meaning."

"The symbol won't be in the legend. It's rarely used, according to the Iron Horse engineer. I saw one on an old map he had for Nevada and asked its meaning."

Creighton tapped the symbol on the map that couldn't have been more than ten miles from their location.

The C in C was becoming perturbed. "Well? What in the hell is it!"

Creighton looked up, beaming with his discovery. "If I'm not mistaken . . . it's a railroad tunnel that runs *through* the mountain!"

0230.

Benhaddou tugged hatefully at the rope holding his prisoner. He enjoyed feeling the twitch at the other end; the way he must have appeared to twitch in his cell while his captors watched him on the television monitor.

Captain Alissa Breen sat on the floor of a cave, not certain where she was, except she knew she was no longer in the hospital tent where this dreadful man had kidnapped her.

The only pleasure she had was in remembering how angered he had become when the motorcycle he had secreted in the hills had stopped running only minutes after he had dragged her to its hiding place. He had ranted and raved in several languages, including English.

That was when he had begun dragging her along the rocky hillside, showing no forgiveness when she had stumbled.

Her leg ached; her head hurt where he had slapped her when she had refused to rise from the ground. How she had managed to travel this far was beyond her reasoning at the moment.

Looking around, she saw that the cave had been lived in over the years. There was the smell of something else in the cave. A burning, distasteful smell.

Bats!

She didn't actually smell them since she wouldn't know their odor from that of a frog. But she heard them; then saw them streaking through the air overhead. Their images flashed past, mostly shadows created by the small fire burning in the center of what appeared to be a giant cavern inside the mountain. A natural chimney had been weathered upward through the cavern, allowing for an escape for the smoke.

Then she saw the light dance off the wall. Something shone brightly for a moment, then was gone, erased by the darkness. Moments later, the image reappeared. It was an animal. A white animal.

A white rhino.

Like the two rhinos in the reserve. That was when she realized where she was. She had heard Jean Peterson talk about the old man and that he lived in a cave. Jean had visited the cave on one occasion. Which meant they weren't far from the reserve. But how could she alert them to her presence?

Benhaddou rose and walked over to where she watched him defiantly. He appeared proud, reminding her of Shona. Except where Shona exuded an aura of compassion, this man gave off the aura of hatred.

"Get some sleep," he said in nearly perfect English. "Tomorrow morning we will begin our journey."

She watched him sit by the fire. He warmed his hands carefully over the flames.

"Where are we going?"

"To your flying machine."

For the first time in her life, Captain Alissa Breen felt the stabbing agony of pure fear!

★★★★★★★★★★★★★

Chapter
Fifty-nine

★★★★★★★

0330.

The mountain had kept its secret better than Creighton had thought possible when he began the search along the base. He found nothing to indicate that a tunnel existed. Not railroad tracks from more than a hundred years ago that would lead directly to the throat of the tunnel. Not a gravel bed.

Nothing.

He was riding in the turret, standing up while watching through his night vision binoculars. He was now in direct communication with the surveying engineer stationed at end of track via the GroundStar network that was now operational.

Which meant he knew about the fire at the reserve, and the kidnapping of Alissa. The identity of the kidnapper was unknown. Clayton speculated it was a Marauder special ops team sent to bring her to the airplane in order to learn its operation.

This brought the current mission to an even greater height of importance: AfriKorps had to get to the encampment and destroy the aircraft. In Clayton's mind the aircraft—if it could be duplicated and if the Marauders could learn to operate it—was worth a dozen divisions.

Creighton agreed.

"Look for a rock face. Or what might appear to be rock. Concrete. That will be the entrance. There may be stress fractures, since the opening hasn't been maintained for over a century."

The voice from 300 miles away was giving him instructions, but in the dense foliage covering the base of the mountain range, the engineer may as well have been telling Creighton that the optimum method for finding a needle in a haystack was to sit on the needle.

"We're in the general area. That much I know. But finding the exact point of the tunnel entrance is damned near impossible. There's too much overgrowth. The night vision capability won't distinguish cracks from tree-branch shadows. Debris has slid down from the mountain, covering much of the base," Creighton reported to the C in C.

Five hundred meters away, Colonel Clayton was in a frazzle. "Goddammit!" He punched in the connection on his boom mike so hard he nearly destroyed the device.

All seemed lost when the Chariot's gunner offered a novel suggestion. "Why don't we recon by fire?"

"What do you mean?" Creighton asked.

Puhaly took sixty seconds to explain his plan. Creighton relayed the plan to the C in C.

"Damn," replied Clayton. "Do you think it'll work?"

"Hell . . . I'd piss on a spark plug if I had one . . . and thought it'd work. We're desperate for anything." Creighton sounded exhausted.

Clayton switched to the all-net frequency and gave his instructions to the MBT's in Lion squadron.

Fifteen minutes later, the thirty tanks were sitting on-line twenty meters apart, covering nearly a quarter mile of the base of the mountain range. The heavy 120mm cannons were trained on the base. When penetrating SABOT rounds had been loaded into the breeches, Creighton gave the order. "Fire!" The ground shook at the base of the mountain range as thirty 120mm cannons unloaded their ordnance into the mountain. The SABOT rounds punched a hole through whatever resistance they met, then an explosive charge followed, blowing a larger, gaping hole through the target zone. The explosions created one continuous eruption of rock, trees, and sand that had lain undisturbed for nearly a century.

"Lase dead ahead," Colonel Clayton ordered.

The laser rangefinders on the thirty MBT's immediately shot straight along the line of fire followed by the SABOTs.

Clayton listened as each MBT tank commander reported a similar readout. The rangefinders were reporting back nearly precisely the distance before firing, indicating the rounds had met sheer resistance.

"Echelon right. Fire when ready," Colonel Clayton ordered.

The ground shook again as the tanks unleashed a deadly fusillade against the mountain base.

"Lase dead ahead," Clayton ordered.

The reports came back negative. Twenty-nine reports. Clayton waited for the thirtieth tank to report: Ribald's Chariot. In the gunner's seat, Puhaly re-lased. When he looked at the digital readout the numbers read 8888, indicating a negative laser range. It was as though he was ranging a target on the other side of the world. Or a hole through the mountain that extended far beyond the 8,000 yard maximum range capability.

"Colonel Clayton . . . Ribald's Chariot reporting negative lase back. I think we've found our tunnel."

"Captain . . . give Sergeant Puhaly my compliments. Then get the hell busy clearing out that tunnel! We've got a battle to fight!"

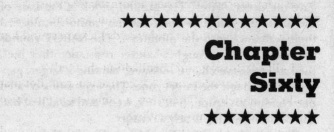

Chapter Sixty

★★★★★★★

Benhaddou heard the cracking sound of the rock as it skipped across the hard floor of the cave. He jerked awake, sat upright, then looked around. From above him, the White Rhino painted on the wall over a century ago stared hauntingly at him. Then there was the second rock. The sharp report echoed through the cavern, sounding like the cracking of bones.

Benhaddou jerked the rope, waking Alissa. He jerked her to her feet.

"What's happening?" The fatigue and pain clouded her brain. It wasn't until she heard a familiar voice that she understood they were no longer alone.

"Captain Breen. This is Roman Standish." From beyond the main tunnel leading to the cave the philosopher's voice rolled through the cavern.

Benhaddou, who spoke and understood English, clamped his hand around her mouth. "You old fool. I will kill her if you come closer."

Benhaddou's eyes roamed the entrance. Momentarily, he saw the white of Roman's toga appear at the narrow entrance. Then more people appeared. Ibo, holding his club. Jean Peterson, her clothes covered with grime from fighting the fire. Neshu, who held a long spear. And five soldiers led by an army officer. All carried automatic weapons.

Benhaddou shifted his grip from around Alissa's mouth to her throat. His huge hands locked around her neck.

"I will kill this woman!" Benhaddou shouted.

Roman stepped forward. "Of course you can. But that would be senseless." There was a calmness in his voice that Benhaddou found unsettling.

The soldiers eased into the cavern and positioned themselves along the wall at the entrance.

Roman's gentle eyes fell on Alissa. "Are you all right, my dear?"

She couldn't speak, except with her eyes. She blinked slowly.

Roman looked again at Benhaddou. "There's no way out of here. You are surrounded." He looked back at the soldiers, who trained their automatic weapons on the Morocc. "They won't let you out of here alive."

"I will kill the woman," he barked.

"And kill yourself in the process," Roman calmly replied. "But there is another way. If you're willing to listen."

Benhaddou's grip didn't relax. "Speak your words, old man."

"We think we know why you've come here. You were sent by the Marauders to bring the woman to their camp. She is the only person who can fly the airplane. But there's something you don't know."

Benhaddou's chin thrust upward, indicating Roman should continue.

"Colonel Clayton is preparing to attack the Marauder encampment and lay siege until they surrender. Therefore, your mission here is meaningless. The woman no longer has any value to you . . . except as a bargaining chip."

Benhaddou replied hatefully, "You lie!"

Roman stepped closer. "You know I don't lie."

Benhaddou knew that was the truth. At his trial the old man had defended him when no other would speak in his defense. He knew the old man did not lie.

"What do you offer?"

"It's quite simple. You release the girl and you will be taken by escort to the south where you'll be set free. You won't be given weapons. You'll be given food and water for three days. That and nothing more. Otherwise, we will leave this cave and you have no means of escaping. There's only one way in . . . one way out."

"I will kill the woman." He said the words as though they were important. But in Roman's face he saw something: the old man knew that risking Alissa's life was the only means he had of saving her.

"You will kill her anyway. And we both know how you enjoy killing women. I won't allow her to suffer that sort of death. If she's to die . . . she'll die here. Among her people. A quick, painless death. Either by your strong hands . . . or the bullets of these soldiers. Either way . . . she won't leave this cave with you."

Benhaddou chuckled throatily. "You are a shrewd old man."

"Not shrewd. Practical. The woman alive is more important to us than seeing you dead. It's a matter of priority. Besides . . . if I know you, you'll turn up again. Our forces will hunt you down and return you to your prison cell. But for now you'll have life—and freedom."

Benhaddou started forward with Alissa. Roman stiffened and extended his hand, indicating the Morocc should stop his advance.

"But—" Roman warned in a voice harder than Benhaddou imagined possible from the old man. "If you try to leave with her—you will both be shot."

Roman raised his hand. The soldiers took aim at the Morocc.

"We won't allow you to take her from this cave." Roman's steady voice warned.

Neshu walked to Roman's side. The glare from her eyes was as hateful as any Benhaddou had ever seen from a man. Except for Ibo, who followed Neshu, holding the long club with the shiny shaft. He glanced at the painting of the White Rhino on the wall, then spoke to Benhaddou in a language both understood.

Benhaddou listened to Ibo.

"You have nothing to lose except your life, which, at this moment, is worth nothing. You have only your hatred to keep you in this place. Release the young woman and leave in peace. Or die in this cavern, never again to see the sun rise or the moon drift across the sky."

The siege in the cave ended with Benhaddou's fingers slowly releasing their grip around Alissa's neck. She pulled herself free and stumbled toward Roman as the soldiers closed in on the Morocc. The officer leading the squad raised his pistol as if to fire.

"No!" commanded Roman. "We have given him our word."

The young officer looked incredulously at the philosopher. "You can't be serious! Colonel Clayton will hang us both if we let this murderous bastard go free."

Roman spoke gently, but with firmness. "He will be escorted to the south by your platoon. I will explain to Colonel Clayton."

"What will you tell Captain Creighton?" the officer asked.

Roman smiled softly. "That his revenge will have to wait until another time. That my responsibility is to the living."

The officer lowered his pistol.

0500.

Colonel Clayton rode standing in the turret; in the distance he could see the string of searchlights burning from the turrets of the advancing MBT's moving through the tunnel toward the opposite side of the mountain range.

Creighton had gone ahead of the main element, scouting the tunnel to the opposite entrance. What he found in the tunnel was what Clayton had hoped: it was relatively clear. Carved through rock harder than concrete, the tunnel had remained intact since it was last used before the Cataclysm.

Some debris had fallen along the course of the rusted railroad tracks, which now splintered like glass beneath the treads of the MBTs, but the core of the tunnel was sound.

Reaching the opposite side, Creighton found nothing but overgrowth blocking the tunnel, concealing the entrance. Ribald's Chariot had punched through to the other side like a knife cutting through warm butter.

Clayton's MBT pushed through to where the other MBT's were turning right and left in an on-line formation. Rolling to a halt beside the Chariot, Clayton looked at his map. A series of hills sat between their position and the Marauder encampment.

Creighton climbed aboard the C in C's MBT and listened to his final orders.

"Your squadron consists of six platoons with six tanks per platoon. Break them down into three elements of two platoons each." His finger ran along the horseshoe-shaped line of hills overlooking the enemy encampment. "When you're in position we'll begin the siege. I'll hold the headquarters and IFV elements in reserve."

Creighton went back to the Chariot and gave orders to the tank commanders over the radio. Like giant turtles, the thirty MBT's went to chameleon mode and full stealth. Laser rangefinding would be absorbed by the skin of the tanks; visual sighting would be impossible as the tanks literally turned the color of the sky and terrain.

Clayton spoke into the boom mike. "Captain Armbrust . . . Lion squadron is moving on-line. What is your situation?"

Armbrust reported his Panther squadron was at the pass at the south end of the valley. "The Marauders are bottled up from this end. There's been no contact."

Creighton climbed down from the turret and went back toward a high outcropping of massive boulders. He climbed to the top of the largest boulder where he raised his night vision binoculars to his eyes. Approximately eight miles below lay the hills behind which the MBT's would take up their defilade positions guns down, turrets protected. Below the hills the enemy encampment could be seen. Adjusting the binoculars to full power, he scanned the interior of the encampment. Rows of Leopard tanks sat in deep defensive bunkers. Infantry elements were dispersed among the armor.

His eyes stopped suddenly as he made out the unmistakable image of Thunder One.

Chapter
Sixty-two

★★★★★★★★

0600.

Major Vita Slazenger was buttoning her blouse in her tent when the first volley of incoming 120mm cannon fire began its deadly waltz through the front row of Leopard tanks. Tank commanders and gunners had been sleeping on the ground beside their tanks, therefore they hadn't been alerted by the telltale chirp as the MBT gunners had activated the laser rangefinders, precisely targeting the Leopards.

Puhaly squeezed off the first round, striking a Leopard on the front row with a SABOT round.

The discarding SABOT, as it is called, is a multi-pieced round assembled around a long bolt made of depleted uranium, designed to penetrate the densest metal. When the bolt penetrates the hull of an enemy tank, it disintegrates, turning into a hailstorm of flying metal debris. The receiving tank is literally shredded on the inside; human occupants rarely escape the deadly shrapnel.

Prior to firing, Puhaly and the other thirty gunners of Lion squadron punched in the lased targets into the multi-targeting computer, giving the thirty tanks full coverage of the entire Marauder armored division.

The gunners had to do nothing more than sit back

and watch the show once the computer selected the target and locked on it with computerized accuracy—stationary or on the move. The computer reloaded and discarded the spent shell automatically, leaving Puhaly to the 7.62 co-axial machine guns, which he began firing with deadly effect at the entrenched infantry units.

"You bastards!" Puhaly shouted with glee. He sighted on an enemy bunker filled with infantry troops and pressed the trigger.

A stream of bullets, every fifth one a golden-tipped tracer, left the co-axial machine guns of the tank and hit the human targets inside the encampment.

Up top, standing in the turret, Creighton was behind the 30mm chain gun, firing steadily at mechanized units that frantically tried to mount up troops and race through the main gate to engage the AfriKorps in the open. None reached the main gate, and within minutes the wreckage began to stockpile in the few avenues the Marauders had left for themselves.

"Focus on the entry points to Thunder One." Clayton's voice came over the radio.

A heavy concentration of 120mm cannon fire began waltzing a twelve-foot-wide groove through the minefields at three separate points. Once the groove reached the inside of the camp, the cannons concentrated on the Leopards and other mechanized units still operational. Huge fireballs erupted as the combination of SABOT and high-explosive HEAT rounds ignited the tanks, turning the Leopards into burning hulks.

Through his binoculars, Clayton saw men running with their clothes aflame; he saw turrets torn from hulls, sent flying through the air as if they were paper plates.

When he saw the groove was prepared for Thunder One, Clayton keyed the mike and gave his order. "Mount up the special ops team."

From behind the hillock, Creighton's Ribald's Chariot plunged up and over as he gave his order. "Assume attack speed. Fast forward. IFV drop into the slot. Lorry take up rear position. Puhaly . . . kick some ass!"

The three war machines stormed toward the groove leading to the interior of the camp.

Chapter Sixty-three

★★★★★★★★

"Like shooting fish in a barrel," Clayton said to himself as he saw the MBT's continue to unleash their steady fire into the encampment. The Marauder camp was ablaze from the petrol depot hit by HEAT rounds in the opening fusillade. A cloud of thick, black smoke rose, flattened, then pressed back to earth, nearly obscuring the camp.

His field glasses switched to the south where he could see a dozen Leopards racing for the southern pass in Green Gate.

"Panther leader . . . twelve bandits en route to your target."

Seconds later he saw the twelve Leopards begin to explode; thick columns of smoke marked their point of destruction against the horizon.

Clayton shifted the glasses to the center of the camp. He saw Thunder One. The aircraft was no longer surrounded by walking guards. But he did see something that made his stomach tighten.

Pressing the switch on the boom mike, Clayton calmly ordered, "Protect Thunder One. Sapper is closing on the aircraft. Repeat. Sapper closing on aircraft."

From that distance Clayton couldn't tell what kind of soldier was racing toward Thunder One. But he did recognize the weapon carried by the soldier.

A shoulder-mounted rocket launcher!

Chapter
Sixty-four

★★★★★★★

Major Vita Slazenger ran drunkenly toward Thunder One. She was carrying a rocket launcher; her hair was almost completely burned from her head. Blood streamed from her ears where the noise had ruptured the eardrums in the wakening moments of the barrage. Her clothes were blackened, burned to tatters.

"Help me," a voice cried. She barely heard the plea, but stopped to look at the headquarters tent.

General Burril was in his underwear. His chest was covered with blood. Then she saw the gaping hole that ran from his left nipple to his armpit.

"Slazenger. Help me . . . you bitch!" Burril ordered.

Slazenger's lips curled evilly as the general fell at her feet. His hand gripped her leg.

"Fuck you, old man. You've destroyed us all!" She kicked him in the chest. Blood spurted from the wound where the white bone of his rib cage was flayed open, revealing his lungs.

She turned and started for Thunder One. She had nothing else to give except that she would not lose her prize! Burril's voice called again as she released the safety mechanism on the launcher.

That was when a staccato of gunfire rippled through the air. She turned to see a stream of gold snake toward Burril and lift his body into the air, where he shook like a rag doll caught in a lion's mouth. Burril fell lifeless to the ground, his eyes open, his mouth slack, drooling blood.

The stream continued on-line. Past the stream she saw one of the American tanks. Turning to face it, she sighted on the front of the hull. Her finger was closing on the trigger when the stream of golden bullets caught her in the belly, then sternum, throat, and between the eyes.

Her back exploded and her brains flew in a thousand directions as her body lifted off the ground, carried by the impact. She slammed to the ground. Her eyes were empty of life but they stared at the strangely shaped prize she had shot from the sky.

She lay dead near the landing gear as a shadow began to form where the sunlight rode over Thunder One.

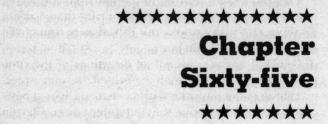

★★★★★★★★★★★★
Chapter
Sixty-five
★★★★★★★

Ribald's Chariot rolled to a halt near Thunder One as Falken's IFV slid alongside. The lorry followed, moving quickly as planned.

The IFV emptied twelve hard-core special operations infantry soldiers who set up a perimeter around the aircraft.

The sergeant driving the lorry swerved inside the perimeter and stopped near the aircraft. Two soldiers scurried out from the cab and began attaching a cable around the fuselage. It took less than two minutes for the cable to be attached and secured. The winch was started; Thunder One rose again into the sky. "Reno!" Creighton shouted over the din inside the camp. Falken turned to see a squad of Marauder soldiers charging. Falken's men moved instinctively, shifting their field of fire to concentrate on the attackers. Puhaly started firing with the co-axial; Creighton was firing from behind the light machine gun on the turret. A storm of gunfire erupted, concentrated on the area beyond Thunder One. The Marauders fell as the deadly wall of flying steel shredded their bodies in an instant.

"Let's mount up!" Creighton ordered.

Ribald's Chariot swung out and turned, followed by the lorry with the IFV taking up the rear.

Creighton kept on firing to the left from the turret, which was swung right. Puhaly was firing the co-axials. To the rear, the IFV troops and Falken were firing from the front, rear, and side ports.

Deadly firepower covered all directions of the compass, cutting a swath through the twisted, burning wreckage; through the human resistance that was light at best.

On the hillock above the Marauder camp, Clayton grinned as he saw the rescue column emerge from the carpet of black smoke covering the battlefield.

He spoke in a whisper over the radio to Creighton. "Good job . . . my brave son."

Chapter Sixty-six

★★★★★★★★

Two days after the battle at Green Gate, Ibo sat on the hillside above the reserve, which Dr. Peterson had named the Equinox Game Reserve in honor of Neshu's tribe; a tribe now lost to oblivion. Below, the animals were spread along the valley, each species establishing its own territory.

His thoughts drifted to the White Rhino. To Adam, who was charred and murdered during the fire. To Eve, who now wandered about alone, except for the small rememberance of Adam she now carried in her womb. Many of the animals had been determined pregnant, and like people, were experiencing the change created by the life-bearing responsibility. The females stayed to themselves. The males wandered and rooted around in their electronically restricted territory. He rose, leaning on his club, noting the flash of sunlight dancing off the metal. He started toward his cave, then stopped. He looked out over the valley and saw that peace had returned. He had weathered the Cataclysm. He had new friends. He was the caretaker of this piece of God's earth.

Life was good.

Chapter Sixty-seven

★★★★★★★★

Creighton and Alissa walked along the edge of the military camp which was now designated AfriKorps Forward. Patrols from Panther squadron were combing the Green Gate valley for remnants of the Marauder division. Little resistance was being encountered.

"What will you do now?" Alissa asked. She slipped her hand into Creighton's.

He felt embarrassed, as though he were betraying the love of his wife. Then he remembered the letter. He knew she would understand.

"I'll be returning to the field. What about you?"

"Colonel Clayton has assigned me to the GroundStar project." She laughed. "He wants me to become gradually oriented before flying over enemy territory."

They looked up as they saw Roman approach.

He looked at Creighton. "May we talk . . . alone?"

Alissa pulled away and went to where Thunder One was parked. She knew about the conversation Roman and TC were going to have. The philosopher thought she should know. After he had ensured Benhaddou's release into the mountains, he told her the truth that two men would ultimately have to face.

"I wish to speak with you about your father," Roman began carefully.

TC shrugged. His father was dead. He was a hero to the people of the Vegas Biosphere. There was nothing more he needed to know.

"What's there to say? He's dead."

Roman looked deep into Creighton's eyes. His white-haired head shook. "No, my son. He's not dead," he said gently. "The man you think is your father is dead. Your real father is alive."

Creighton felt as though he had been kicked in the stomach. "What the hell do you mean?"

Roman explained. "Many years ago, before you were born, your mother fell in love with a young soldier in the DESFOR. She wanted to marry him, but the genetic testing proved inconclusive regarding the offspring. That was a paramount consideration to ensure that genetic breeding was not compromised by the slightest possibility of incest. Therefore, she was denied permission to marry the man. Instead, she married another young man. A fine young man. A young officer named Creighton."

Creighton looked stunned. "What are you saying?" He felt his fists ball into two hardened tongs.

Roman's voice was soft. "I'm saying the man you think was your father is not your natural father."

Creighton's face was now hard as steel. His eyes burned at the philosopher. "Explain yourself, damn you!"

Roman continued. "The love your mother had for the other officer was no secret. Gradually, her husband learned the truth. That she loved another man. This changed him. He became cold. Cruel. Some thought it was this hatred that turned him into such an exemplary soldier. He showed no fear. It was as though he knew no fear. I knew different. He grew to hate everything and took out that hatred on the hostiles. The same hatred that ultimately led to his death."

"What happened?"

"It was no great secret. All one had to do was look at Captain Creighton. He was blond, with flashing blue eyes. Like your mother."

Creighton was dark haired. His eyes were brown. "My mother had an affair with the man she couldn't marry?"

"Love will inevitably cause certain situations. As he became more cruel she was drawn to the one man who gave her love and kindness. She became pregnant. A few years after your birth, Captain Creighton led a patrol into the desert. He never returned. Only one man returned. The officer your mother loved. There was a great deal of speculation over what happened. The surviving officer never said a word except that Captain Creighton died a hero fighting the hostiles."

Creighton began to piece together the puzzle. "You're saying the other officer killed my father!"

Roman shrugged. "There was never any formal investigation regarding that possibility. However, I will say this . . . knowing Captain Creighton . . . and the other officer, if there was a confrontation it was initiated by Captain Creighton. The other officer would have only acted in self-defense. He's a very honorable man."

TC looked seriously at Roman. "Let's cut through the cryptic bullshit, Roman. I want an answer. A straight answer. Who is the officer you claim is my father!"

Roman released a long sigh and replied, "Colonel Thomas Clayton."

Epilogue

★★★★★★★

Base Camp One. AfriKorps Headquarters.

Colonel Thomas Clayton stood at the grave site, surrounded by dozens of graves holding brave men and women he had brought from the other side of the world to die in a foreign land.

Three days had passed since the battle at Green Gate. Now another confrontation lay ahead. It would begin soon. He checked his watch. The Iron Horse would have arrived thirty minutes ago, carrying its angry passenger.

He waited where he knew he should. In this place of heroes. To talk with a hero about another hero.

To talk about truth.

He heard a hum; he didn't look back as the Landrover slid to a halt. Moments later, he heard the hurried footsteps approaching from the rear. Then he heard the voice he was expecting.

"Turn around you sonofabitch!"

He turned to the sun-bronzed face of Captain Abraham Creighton. To the pistol trained on his forehead.

"Good afternoon, captain."

"Don't be polite. I don't like to shoot polite sons-abitches."

The colonel plunged his hands into his pockets. He

wasn't wearing a weapon. He had been warned by Roman that Creighton was driving his MBT like a wild man toward end of track to catch the train to Base Camp One. He had had more than a day to prepare for the confrontation. A day to think of what he would say. He never found the words.

"You've come here for something important to you. I can understand that. But you should consider the consequences first. Your life will be ruined. Your career destroyed. You'll spend the rest of your life in a prison cell."

"I've thought about that." He looked at the grave of his wife. A cactus rose blossomed; placed there by Hamp Floris the day of her funeral.

"I don't think you have." He laughed. "You thought about nothing but betrayal. And revenge."

"I've thought about the bastard who's destroyed my life."

"You are the only person who can destroy your life. You and you alone."

Tears formed in Creighton's eyes. "You could have left us alone. We could still be in the Western Quadrant." He pointed at the grave. "She'd still be alive!"

Clayton shook his head. He reached into his pocket and withdrew a folded piece of paper. "No. She wouldn't be alive. Not now."

He extended his hand to Creighton, offering the proof of his statement. Then he continued. "Last year, when I was assigned the command of AfriKorps, Silver came to me and showed me that report. It's a medical report. Read for yourself."

He read the report. His face turned ashen. "She was dying?"

Clayton nodded. "She was a physician. She contracted

the disease from one of the hostiles she was treating in the hospital. The disease was incurable. She had approximately a year to live."

"Why didn't she tell me?"

"She knew you would have refused to come to Africa."

He didn't understand. "Why was that important?"

"You damn fool. You're blind to everything. She wanted to be with her family! With you. With me. We were all the family she had left. She wanted you to know your natural father. She said she wanted to have your child. My grandchild! She wanted us together!"

Creighton was stunned. "You mean she knew? About you and my mother? About me!"

Clayton laughed. "Of course she knew. Everyone in the Vegas Biosphere knew . . . except you."

TC felt foolish. "Why didn't you tell me?"

Clayton looked ashamed. "I couldn't. She was going to tell you when the time was right."

TC's voice broke. "She never got the chance."

Clayton turned and faced the grave of Silver Allenbey-Creighton. "She made me promise to pull all the strings to get you two married before we left the United States. I had to call in a big favor. It was President Dawson who gave the final approval."

"I didn't know." TC slipped the pistol into his holster. He stepped to the grave and knelt. His fingers touched the cactus rose.

"What now?" Creighton asked.

"We go forward. Life goes on. We have a job to complete."

"What about you and I? I still blame you for her death."

"I know. I feel the same way. I don't mind. Someone has to bear the burden somewhere along the line. It certainly wasn't her fault. Not your fault either."

Captain Abraham Creighton stood and walked back to the Landrover. He said nothing more.

Colonel Thomas Clayton stood in silence as he watched his son drive away, leaving him with the silence of the graveyard.

With the loneliness of his memories.

BILL DOLAN is the pseudonym of an author who lives in North Dakota. He is a Vietnam veteran and has written several previous novels.